WEALTH AND INEQUALITY IN BRITAIN

HISTORICAL HANDBOOKS

WEALTH AND INEQUALITY IN BRITAIN

W. D. RUBINSTEIN

faber and faber

LONDON · BOSTON

First published in 1986
by Faber and Faber Limited
3 Queen Square London WC1N 3AU

Printed in Great Britain by
Redwood Burn Ltd Trowbridge Wiltshire
All rights reserved

British Library Cataloguing in Publication Data

Rubinstein, W.D.
Wealth and Inequality in Britain – (Historical
handbooks)
1. Social classes – Great Britain – History –
20th century   2. Great Britain – Economic
conditions – 1945–
I. Title   II. Series
305.5′0941   HN400.S6
ISBN 0-571-13924-8

Library of Congress Cataloging in Publication Data

Rubinstein, W.D.
Wealth and inequality in Britain.
(Historical handbooks series) (Faber paperbacks)
Bibliography: p.
1. Wealth – Great Britain – History.
2. Income distribution – Great Britain – History.
I. Title   II. Series
HC260.W4R83 1986   339.2′2′0941   86-2092
ISBN 0-571-13924-8 (pbk.)

CONTENTS

Acknowledgements

The figures on pages 60 and 61 and the tables on pages 62 and 67 are taken from Lee Soltow, 'Long-Run Changes in British Income Inequality' in A.B. Atkinson (ed) *Wealth, Income, and Inequality*, (2nd edn), published by Oxford University Press, 1980, and reproduced by permission of the publisher.

The figure on page 119 is taken from Guy Routh, *Occupation and Pay in Great Britain 1906–79*, published by The Macmillan Press Limited, 1980, and reproduced by permission of the publisher.

Tables and Figures

Tables

Figures

Preface

Despite two hundred years of gradual but perhaps fundamental reform, British society remains one in which very marked degrees of economic inequality seem to persist. This book is an attempt to chart the evolution of economic inequality in Britain, focusing centrally on inequalities in wealth and income.

Necessarily an examination of economic inequality must lead to more basic questions of social stratification, and these will be touched upon as well. In particular the contrast between the evolutionary patterns of economic and political equality in Britain over the past two hundred years will be discussed and examined. At its heart, however, this is a book about economic inequality in modern Britain, and how the distribution of wealth and income has ·changed, the reasons for this evolution, and its implications for British society.

The subject of wealth and inequality is one about which most people have strong views, often preconceived, and it is doubtful whether any study of this subject can be truly neutral. This is not so much because of the nature of the statistics and evidence – although the data are by no means as clear-cut as for many other topics in economic history – as because of the interpretation one may place on the evidence, via which one man's very nearly empty glass may quickly become, for another man, very nearly full. Although in this work I have gathered a wide range of historical evidence, mainly statistical, which is as 'objective' as it can be, some will doubtless question my conclusions. In particular it may be said that I have paid insufficient attention to the abundant evidence of Britain's economic failure during the past four decades – a failure increasing exponentially, it seems, with the passage of time – but have especially ignored the tragic human costs of this failure, above all for the unemployed.

There are two responses one might make to this, apart from saying in advance that one is well aware that this may seem to be so. First, this is a work of history and is, in particular, an attempt to answer 'how Britain came to be what it is', and today's situation must always be seen here in light of the past. Secondly, although the manifold and lamentable failings of the British economy have been proclaimed innumerable times in every conceivable forum, one hears of its successes rather less often. It will become apparent from this work that Britain's record in terms of living standards and wealth distribution since 1945 contrasts so markedly with her relative failure in most other key economic areas that the novelty alone justifies focusing on them. It is, indeed, indicative of the position to which Britain has come that one feels compelled to apologize for focusing on them at all.

Among the debts I incurred in writing this work, I must thank Professor F.M.L. Thompson and Dr Avner Offer, the editors of this series, for their encouragement and advice, my colleagues Roy Hay and Joe Remenyi, and John Piggott of the Australian National University, for their helpful bibliographical references. In particular I should also thank Mrs Jenny Hayes and the other secretaries of the School of Social Sciences at Deakin University for word processing the manuscripts so efficiently.

W.D. Rubinstein

I

Introduction

More than most public issues, questions of economic equality affect each of us at several different levels. Each of us is a participant in the economic system and is in receipt of an income (however meagre). Normally, we all have hopes and ambitions for the acquisition of property and of an income sufficient to purchase the 'good things of life'. Even if we may reject the hedonism of such desires, we must nevertheless recognize that the continuing success of modern society depends very significantly upon the maintenance of a successful economy, and this necessarily entails the addressing of questions of economic equality and inequality.

Increasingly, too, issues of economic inequality and distribution are at the heart of contemporary political debate. Indeed, one may go beyond this to make two more sweeping and far-reaching claims: in Britain (and elsewhere) in this century nearly all domestic political issues of consequence have revolved around questions of economic distribution, and since the Edwardian period – if not before – the major political parties have been centrally organized around their attitude to economic distribution, with left-wing parties, especially Labour, typically advocating more far-reaching measures of economic equality.

More specifically, many if not most day-to-day political questions and issues, in Britain and elsewhere, may be seen as aspects of the wider and more general question of economic equality. Should the Chancellor raise or lower the income tax? Will the mortgage interest rate rise or fall? Will sterling decline against the dollar and other foreign currencies? Is your rate bill to increase yet again? All of these, and many other such questions, may be seen at least in part as issues of economic equality and inequality, for their answers economically advantage some individuals or groups in the population while disadvantaging others. Changes in the income tax, or in the interest rate, or in the value of sterling may eventually produce a greater or lesser degree of economic equality throughout the whole of society; certainly they have more far-reaching effects than are evident at first glance. Although the makers of British economic policy have many motives in arriving at the policies which they adopt, quite possibly – and increasingly – one major consideration is the effect these policies will have on the overall distribution of wealth and income.

Clearly, questions of income and wealth distribution are more than straightforward questions of everyday politics; indeed, they are more than economic questions. They are also questions of morality and ethics, as well as of basic political ideology. Many radicals believe, and many radicals in the past two hundred years have previously believed, often with great passion and conviction, that wealth and income are far too unevenly distributed in British society. In particular, there is a long-standing radical tradition in Britain (and elsewhere) that the rich are too rich and the poor too poor; often the suggestion is that the rich have become rich at the expense of the poor, either in Britain or, internationally, as in the Third World. This tradition is long standing and has waxed and waned on the British left along with the other concerns demonstrated by the left – for greater democracy, for economic growth, for the nationalization of industries, for reform of government and education – over the past two centuries. In contrast, conservatives (and most nineteenth-century or classical liberals) have in general defended the existing distribution of wealth and income as necessary for economic efficiency and for the proper rewarding of entrepreneurial effort and individual skill. Conservatives have long claimed to be in favour of substantially lower taxes and far less government involvement in the economy than are radicals; whether these claims are true can, of course, be debated. Some would argue that conservatives defend the existing inequalities of wealth and income because most conservatives are themselves wealthy or at least affluent, although the substantial number of working-class Tories (side-by-side with middle-class or even wealthy radicals) means that conservative attitudes toward inequality have a far wider appeal than merely to the wealthy.

One may indeed go further than this. Although radicals and conservatives in the modern world tend to differ over a host of issues – conservatives respect traditional institutions, radicals are critical of them; conservatives often tend to be patriotic and 'realistic' over foreign policy, radicals claim to be internationalist, and so on – it is perhaps no exaggeration to claim that the central distinction between today's conservatives and radicals lies in their respective attitudes toward questions of economic equality and its ramifications. Generally, the further left one goes on the political spectrum the more one favours economic equality and the more one opposes the inequalities, especially in the ownership of property, allegedly created by capitalism; conversely, the further right one goes (although the authoritarian far right may be an exception to this), the more reluctant one is deliberately to confiscate or redistribute wealth and income. Indeed, if one had to name a single political issue which most differentiated Labour from the Tories it would be precisely their and their followers' respective attitudes toward economic inequality.

Furthermore, it is now generally believed by radicals in Britain that questions of wealth and income distribution should become much more central to the agenda of the left than has been the case in past decades, when the mainstream of the Labour Party seldom centrally addressed questions of income and wealth equality. At the other end of the political spectrum, many right-wing conservatives now defend greater economic inequality as necessary for economic efficiency and successful entrepreneurship than in the past, while the cutting of direct taxation is a perpetual desire of nearly all conservatives. It is thus probable that questions of economic equality will become much more central to Britain's political agenda than was the case before the past decade or so, especially if the Labour Party continues to be dominated by its ideological left wing.

For all of these reasons, an informed discussion of this question and its implications from the viewpoint of Britain's historical experience seems valuable and necessary. It is the intention of this book to examine the historical experience of economic inequality in Britain, how this has evolved and changed over the past two centuries, and how this evolution is related to other questions of social stratification and political and social equality.

Inequality in historical perspective

Before examining the actual facts, so far as they are known to historians, concerning the historical distribution of wealth and income in Britain, two other matters should be considered. First, we shall examine a number of leading theories of social stratification which sociologists have advanced to explain why inequality exists in society – why it seems to exist in *all* societies – and the clearest way in which stratification should be viewed. From time to time in the text we shall refer to these theories, or to concepts derived from them, in examining economic inequality in Britain. Secondly, we shall need to define many of the basic terms which are used in discussing this subject – both economic terms (like 'income' and 'wealth') and political or quasi-political ones (like the nuances of 'equality' and 'inequality').

Theories of inequality

Because of the seeming ubiquity of inequality in its various forms in all human societies, including the most advanced, classical sociological thought has produced a number of significant theories to explain or account for the persistence of inequality in all societies, including those with democratic governments. Four such theories may be regarded as most general and influential in their application, and should be discussed here, at least briefly.

Before doing so, however, it is necessary to make clear that these are *sociological* theories and do not represent the views of historians. Many historians would be reluctant to attempt theory making at this level of generality, and would be much more concerned to identify the differences and distinctive characteristics of different societies and time periods rather than their common features. Necessarily, too, in 'grand theory' (as such theories are sometimes termed) the detail and nuance which is commonly the substance of much written history is lost, sacrificed in the pursuit of generalized rules common to many societies. Several of these theories, indeed, are deliberately 'ahistorical' – that is, they are seen by their partisans as valid for all societies regardless of their peculiar historical experience.

The first of these sociological theories to be propounded, and probably most influential, is *Marxism*. Karl Marx (1818–83) held that previous history was a ceaseless class struggle between a dominant ruling class and the rest of society. (Selsam, Goldway, and Martel, 25–34, 43–51.) Inequality is thus a natural and ineluctable feature of the class nature of all societies which have previously existed. These previous ruling classes were invariably rooted in, and took their particular nature from, the economic base of that society, with a slave-owning elite characteristic of the ancient world, a feudal aristocracy of the Middle Ages, and capitalist bourgeoisie of the modern European world. Each ruling elite repressed threats to its rule which erupted from below, made laws, religions, and culture which mirrored its particular value system and remained in power either until a new, more economically efficient ruling group successfully challenged its rule (as the bourgeoisie did to the feudal aristocracy in several northern European countries) or until overthrown by revolution (as the French bourgeoisie overthrew the ruling feudal aristocracy in the Revolution of 1789). The Industrial Revolution produced an army of propertyless wage slaves – the urban proletariat who would, according to Marx, eventually overthrow bourgeois society and establish a classless socialist state. To Marx and most Marxists, then, until the triumph of the working class, inequality was and is a pervasive feature of all societies and is based, in the final analysis, in the *economic* domination of society by one ruling class.

Karl Marx and his collaborator Friedrich Engels (1820–95) were both gifted and imaginative historians who were, to an extent possibly not appreciated, sensitive to differences in the evolution and development of particular societies, and were aware of the unique historical features of British society which distinguished its evolution from that of most other European societies. Nevertheless, to them Britain was the earliest example of a bourgeois, industrial society and hence not fundamentally different from other societies which followed Britain on the path to industrial capitalism.

The great German sociologist *Max Weber* (1864–1920) developed a theory of social stratification which differed in a number of essential ways from Marx's. Where Marxism sees the overriding determinant of inequality and stratification in all societies as in essence one-dimensional – economic – in their nature, Weber saw the social hierarchy as multi-dimensional. In particular, Weber (Gerth and Mills, 180–195) differentiated between what he termed class, status, and power ('party' in Weber's original formulation) as conceptually distinct axes of inequality which were not reducible to one another or to a more fundamental dimension of inequality. To Weber, 'class' – an individual's economic position, used in his terminology in a sense similar to that employed by Marx – must be carefully distinguished from the separate concepts of 'status' and 'power'. 'Status' is an individual's (or group's) prestige or standing in the eyes of others. An individual may have a different and contradictory standing when viewed from the perspective of class (economic power) and status (prestige). For instance – to give some examples from nineteenth-century British history – a self-made Methodist cotton spinner from an industrial town might well have been regarded by England's landed aristocrats and gentry of the day as a vulgar upstart and undesirable intruder into the traditional hierarchy of society (status), yet may well have been as rich as they and more significant as an employer of labour and as an entrepreneur (class). Conversely, an Anglican vicar enjoyed unquestioned high status in nineteenth-century England but in many cases earned a comparatively meagre income. Differing from both class and status, according to Weber, is power. By the First World War, neither the landed aristocrat nor the cotton spinner might have been as powerful as a trade union leader of working-class origin, and the most powerful men in the politics of a modern democracy might well be drawn from social classes outside of the traditional hierarchy of wealth and status.

Weber's theory of stratification is particularly valuable for examining the situation which has arisen in many democratic countries in the twentieth century. In them groups have risen in the social and political hierarchy who are, it would surely seem, not a part of the 'bourgeois ruling class' in any direct sense. The most notable of these is, of course, the trade union and Labour elite. Since 1924, the Labour Party – which claims to represent the working class and is committed, at least on paper, to socialism – has formed the Government on six different occasions, twice (1945–50 and 1966–70) with very large parliamentary majorities. Similarly, Britain's trade unions are universally acknowledged to be among the most powerful of organized groups in modern Britain – some would say *the* most powerful – and the TUC has been an important element in bringing down several governments.

Other groups, seemingly not a direct part of an economically wealthy or powerful capitalist class, have also risen to key importance in this century. The Civil Service, the permanent bureaucracy of government, has expanded enormously in size, power, and influence since before the First World War. Technologically knowledgeable academics and advisers of various sorts often occupy key positions in a society which is increasingly reliant on the specialized knowledge of such men. Even the managers of modern corporations (as opposed to the asset-owning tycoons of the past) are often not themselves wealthy and would, it is sometimes argued, continue with very little change if their businesses were nationalized.

By separating the axes of status and power from class or economic position, Weber has, it would seem, put a viewpoint more relevant to the complexities of the twentieth century's democracy than Marxism, and present day Marxists (of various shades and schools) have often gone to great lengths to attempt to fit these complexities into an encompassing Marxist framework. (Miliband *passim*; Poulantzas *passim*; Althusser *passim*.)

To some of the so-called classical sociologists, not merely inequality but the existence of elites is a necessary and persistent feature of all human societies. Although elite groups may alter quite basically in their composition and ideology, they are invariably present in *all* societies and it is naive to expect that any future society can emerge which will not contain a small governing elite. Not surprisingly, we term the sociologists who have held this view *Elitists*, a group which includes such sociological thinkers as Pareto, Mosca, and Michels. The 'elitist' tradition has also been strongly concerned with the so-called 'circulation of elites', the extent to which new governing individuals and groups replace the older ones, and has additionally been concerned with the extent to which successive governing ideologies retain similar or functionally equivalent symbols or myths (the so-called 'residues') which persist in all societies.

No sociologist or historian, it seems, has attempted consistently to apply an 'elitist' perspective to modern British history[1] yet, as with a Weberian approach, Britain's history might apparently provide fertile ground for such an approach. The persistence of aristocratic rule into the twentieth century, the seeming cooption of rival elites like the nineteenth-century industrialists, and the continuing inequalities in many aspects of British society despite the coming of democracy, might easily be seen as fitting into an 'elitist' framework. Far less clear, however, is the growing necessity for small elites to respond to the pressures created by non-elite groups in any modern democracy. The composition of and the relationship between the various elements which might be seen as constituting a part of the British elite – are trade unions, for example, such an element? – must similarly be clarified in any 'elitist' view of stratification and power in Britain.

The three preceding perspectives have in common emphasized the existence and persistence of elites and inequalities without directly focusing upon their utility for society. Some American sociologists of the so-called *Functionalist* school have seen inequality not as rooted in the attempt by one group to achieve and maintain power at the expense of the majority, but in the functional necessity in all modern societies for its most important offices and positions to be filled by its most competent personnel. This view was put most notably by the American sociologists Davis and Moore who argued that

> Social inequality is . . . an unconsciously evolved device by which societies insure that the most important positions are conscientiously filled by the most important persons. Hence every society, no matter how simple or complex, must differentiate between persons in terms of both prestige and esteem, and must therefore possess a certain amount of institutionalized inequality. (Davis and Moore, 243)

Among these dimensions of 'institutionalized inequality', salary and other monetary rewards are of course the most important, but a host of others ranging from office size to holiday time are also among the ways that executives and directors of modern organizations are distinguished from ordinary workers.

A 'functionalist' view of power is clearly likely to be more plausible when examining the modern corporation and other institutions with a 'rational' hierarchical structure. In a number of crucial respects, however, the 'functionalist' view seems to ignore many of the most important dimensions of modern British history and societal organization. Britain remained largely without modern and 'rational' hierarchical structures and institutions until the mid-nineteenth century or even later; previously, rewards and duties were often not congruent and frequently were 'irrational' from a 'functionalist' perspective[2] (Rubinstein, 'Old Corruption', *passim*). More basically, although a 'functionalist' perspective may arguably describe – at least in theory – those institutions with a managerial structure of promotion and reward, in Britain class and economic power have very largely been a result of the inheritance of wealth and, often, of positions of influence or high status. Britain's wealth-

iest men and most important economic elites have thus been chosen
not because they were the 'most qualified' to fill their elite positions,
but because of the sheer accident of birth and inheritance. Even
within institutions with a managerial framework, promotion to
positions of authority has, it is widely perceived, often been limited
to those of at least an upper-middle-class background who have
attended a fee-paying secondary school and university, and who
exhibit the personal attributes, especially the right accent and
correct 'breeding' and manners, of the upper middle class and
above. In the great majority of cases, persons of working-class
background cannot realistically aspire to enter the managerial elite.
Indeed, certain groups, most obviously and rigorously women,
have historically been excluded from entry into the managerial
elites of many institutions, regardless of their abilities or inherent
competence.

Nevertheless, and despite its obvious shortcomings as a comprehensive description of the British social hierarchy, many aspects of
the 'functionalist' viewpoint do provide a useful and significant
insight into the workings of modern hierarchical institutions. It is
probably a feature of most organizations of all sorts in contemporary
society that they increasingly approach, however haphazardly, the
model postulated by 'functionalist' theory. Indeed, much of the
evolution of British society since 1800, including the deliberate
reform of pre-modern governmental institutions and the expansion
of a corporate economy, represents the emergence of organizations
with – at least theoretically – a 'functional' administrative hierarchy. In particular, the vast expansion of the 'white collar' sector
of the economy – office workers and the administrative and clerical
staff of private corporations, the state bureaucracy, and independent institutions of various sorts – may be seen as representing the
growth of functional and rational hierarchies. Within the capitalist
business sector itself the number of independent businessmen, large
and small, has declined in this century while corporations, with
their 'functional' hierarchies, have grown enormously in size and
scope.

Forms of equality and inequality

It is clear from the above discussion of stratification theory that
many sociologists find it useful to look at inequality as a single,

general term embracing a variety of facets within society, not necessarily related. Indeed, the terms 'equality' and 'inequality' are notoriously difficult to define concisely and cogently. Possibly the best way to approach this multi-faceted term for the purpose of this historical survey is to trace the evolution of inequality in four distinct but related spheres: legal, political, social, and economic. Perhaps the most important point which might be made of the historical development of equality in Britain in these spheres is that the evolution of each might well be quite different and distinct. Even if, broadly, there has been a long historical trend to ever greater equality in most areas of society, it is entirely possible that in some of these areas the pattern may be quite different.

Legal equality

By legal inequality is meant the existence of laws which affect one defined class or group in society more adversely than other sections of society. In many European states through the Middle Ages and down to modern times perhaps the most clear-cut instance of this were the laws relating to feudalism and the peasantry, which gave legal sanction to serfdom and the virtual enslavement of a large portion of the rural population. Serfdom existed in France until the Revolution of 1789, in Prussia until 1806, and in Russia until 1861. It has recently been argued that feudalism in any form never existed in England, certainly not since the thirteenth century (MacFarlane *passim*). Whatever the truth of this claim, which is controversial, it is certainly true that Britain imposed fewer legal restrictions on any predefined class of persons than any European society and those which existed were swept away by the various revolutions (from above and below) which have marked British history during the past five centuries. The power and wealth of the pre-Reformation Church was destroyed by Henry VIII; the House of Stuart's attempts at establishing an absolute or quasi-absolute monarchy on the French or Austrian model were stymied by the Civil War and Revolutionary settlement of 1688, and by the power attaching to the landed oligarchy which dominated British politics during the eighteenth century. By the late eighteenth century an apparent consensus had emerged throughout English society that Englishmen were 'free born' and could never, without violating the deepest tenets of its unwritten Constitution, be enslaved. This is affirmed by the famous court ruling of 1772 that slavery could not exist in Britain (although it continued in the British colonies for another sixty years) and that any slave who set foot in Britain automatically became a free man.

Exceptions to the strict principle of legal equality did, of course, exist until the twentieth century, especially if the concept is broadened to include the notion of political equality (discussed below). The right to hold many public offices and to be educated at a university was restricted in England and Wales to male members of the Church of England, with Protestant dissenters, Catholics, Jews, atheists and women granted these rights only at various times in the nineteenth century; additionally, Protestant dissenters and (in particular) Roman Catholics[3] suffered from a variety of other legal restrictions from the seventeenth until the nineteenth centuries. But even these restrictions – for instance, on the right to take one's seat in Parliament if elected – did not represent blanket discrimination against the group concerned in the sense, say, which Jews in Nazi Germany suffered or non-whites in South Africa suffer blanket discrimination as members *per se* of a legally defined group. No laws – except possibly some directed at Roman Catholics – barred members of these groups *per se* from a privilege granted to others; instead, all persons who, for instance, were about to enter (or graduate from) a university were required to swear an oath which only an Anglican could conscientiously make, affirming, via their belief in the Thirty Nine Articles, the Anglican credo. In most cases, non-Anglicans were perfectly free to take this oath unless, of course, they found it intolerably inconsistent with their beliefs. Non-Anglicans who met the property or other franchise qualifications could vote (but see note 3) and non-Anglicans were also fully entitled to own property and to participate in business life. Protestant dissenters and Jews were very prominent in British business life during the period of industrialization, and dissenters, especially Quakers, Congregationalists, and Unitarians, were so prominent that they have been frequently credited by historians with 'sparking' the Industrial Revolution (Flinn, 82–90).

At the top end of the social scale, the British aristocracy was also unique among European aristocracies in commanding very few, if any, special legal privileges. Peers of England and of the United Kingdom, and a certain number of Scottish and Irish peers, could sit and vote in the House of Lords, while peers accused of crimes could, in certain cases, be tried by their 'peers' in the House of Lords rather than by an ordinary jury. Apart from these, the post-medieval British aristocracy had no special legal privileges whatever. In contrast to the situation in France and throughout Europe, they did not have the right to payments of any kind from their 'peasants', there being no British peasants after the Middle Ages. They were exempt from no taxes and normally received no special salaries or payments from the Government as holders of a title, held no special status or privileges in law suits or before the law, and did not *per se* have the right to be appointed to any public office, although aristocrats did comprise the majority of Cabinet ministers and of important local office holders in the counties until this century. Indeed, they were not a 'caste' in the sense of the European nobility, since an aristocratic title was inherited only by the eldest son of a peer, his other children and more distant relatives being commoners with no special legal privileges or status whatever. The British aristocracy was therefore always the smallest in Europe, membership of the House of Lords numbering only 193 peers in 1714, 409 in 1837, and 551 in 1900 (together with 26–30 Anglican bishops and archbishops). In dramatic contrast, because the status of nobility descended by inheritance to all close relatives of a nobleman, France on the eve of the 1789 Revolution contained an estimated 250,000 members of the nobility. Marriage between British aristocrats and commoners was not only not forbidden but was extremely common, especially – at least in proverbial account – between the daughters of wealthy merchants and the sons of peers. Finally, the British aristocracy included the unique orders of baronets (hereditary knights) and knights, who were titled persons but not members of the nobility in the strict sense and intermediate in status between the peerage and the commoners. The conferment of a baronetcy or knighthood, which generally went to landed gentry of the second rank, senior office holders in the bureaucracy, most judges, senior colonial officials and military officers, Lord Mayors of London and other large cities, and the like, gave its holder no special privileges whatever, nor the right to sit in the House of Lords.

To many people, the term 'legal equality' probably connotes the legal system itself. Here too, one may fairly say that England had from surprisingly early evolved a judicial system which was, by any reasonable standards, remarkably fair, with *habeas corpus*, the presumption of the innocence of the accused, trial by jury, an independent and impartial judiciary, strict evidential rules, the right of accused persons to be represented by counsel of their choice, and the outlawing of torture and 'cruel and unusual punishments' well established in English (though not always in Scottish) law from the Glorious Revolution onward, if not from long before. In particular, the strict independence of the judiciary from the executive, and the English jury system, by which guilt and innocence were decided not (as in most of Europe) by a panel of judges but by ordinary laymen, randomly selected, were literally centuries ahead of their time and without parallel in the world of that time in their attempts to achieve even-handedness and justice. The progressive nature of the English judiciary, at least in theory, is probably not sufficiently appreciated today, even by contemporary historians concerned with the savagery of pre-Reform punishment and the alleged class basis of the legal system (Hay, *passim*). As with much in the actual working of Britain's institutions, the fairness in practice of what was, in theory, an even-handed system was marred by the fact that the use of the system was, in the real world, not free, and those who could afford to pay first-rate counsel, or who appeared to be of higher status, obviously had an easier time in any legal dispute than the poor. (The situation of the poor in legal disputes probably worsened during the eighteenth century.) Nevertheless, *compared with* contemporary legal systems elsewhere in the European world, the English judicial process was quite progressive and was, justly, a matter of national pride.

Until the twentieth century, there was one group of persons, numbering half the population, who were often exceptions in a general sense to the principle of equal British justice, namely women. As everyone knows, women could not vote in Parliamentary elections or serve in any except some local offices until 1918, and were rigorously excluded from a host of other rights and privileges, ranging from attendance at universities to training and practice at a profession to jury service, until the later nineteenth century at the earliest, and more normally until after the First World War. There was until that time, if not later, an explicit presumption that husbands and fathers were heads of their families and households, and that women were heads of households, if at all, only in the absence of a male.

As pervasive as this picture of discrimination doubtless was, a number of points ought also to be noted. The differences between males and females, and the essential reason for any distinction between them, were biological in nature rather than based in class or status; so long as it was universally believed that the physiological differences between the sexes 'fitted' each for a 'different role in life', a view seemingly fully endorsed by religion as well as common sense and experience, women were regarded not so much as inferior to men as entirely different; the sense of inferiority which attached to their 'role in life' was due to the fact that the public sphere of governance belonged entirely to the male. Yet the laws *protected* women much as they protected men. Violent crimes against women (apart perhaps from those committed in marriage) were always severely punished; indeed, the special and separate status of women entitled them to special forms of legal protection, for instance in the ownership of property, and it is possibly more helpful and accurate to see the (literally) paternalistic and patronizing nature of the legal status of women as setting them apart from the legal status accorded to men prior to this century, rather than discriminating against them as such. This is borne out by the generally higher legal status (ironically coupled with a lower status in terms of prestige) accorded to spinsters and widows as opposed to married women. While married women automatically surrendered their property rights to their husbands until 1882, spinsters and widows – women heads of households – retained their property rights. Women householders who were ratepayers could also vote in local elections from the 1870s onward and, in elections for the London County Council, were an electoral force of some importance by the early twentieth century.

Then too, compared with virtually any other contemporary society, the legal status of British women was immeasurably superior, a phenomenon which began at the very top of society, with the females who became queens of England in their own right, whereas throughout Europe women were debarred by the so-called Salic Law from reigning in their own right. Such institutions as arranged marriages, child marriage, the forbidding of divorce to women, and the virtual imprisonment of widows, practised in many parts of Europe, were always unknown (and often explicitly forbidden) in Britain, to say nothing of practices like polygamy, *suttee*, female circumcision, female infanticide and similar enormities common throughout most of the non-European world where the status of women frequently resembled (and resembles) that of animals. It is no coincidence that Britain always produced an exceptional number of talented women in areas which were open to women (such as Jane Austen, the Brontë sisters, and George Eliot among writers) or that the movement for women's suffrage and other rights emerged more notably in Britain (and in America) than anywhere else.

The twentieth century has seen the elimination of virtually all examples of legally proscribed and enforced inequalities in Britain. Indeed, it is not easy to think of a single example of rights or actions which are explicitly forbidden to one section of the population and to them alone, the exception to this rule being children and minors. So far has the growth of legal equality come that there are now persistent demands (as practised and enforced in the United States) for 'reverse discrimination' in favour of 'minorities', especially women and blacks, and the situation may well arise in which a new legally *privileged* caste arises from among such groups. At present, the legal rights of such minorities are specially protected by such bodies as the Commission for Racial Equality. It seems highly improbable, barring a far-reaching political transformation, that a section or group could become the target of legally enforced inequality, given Britain's historical and legal traditions and the present climate of opinion.

Political equality

Various aspects of the history of political equality have been discussed in the previous section, but here we must examine such topics as the right to equal participation in the political process – the right to vote and to hold office – the ability of an individual or group to influence the political process after elections have occurred, and the accountability of a government to Parliament and to the electorate.

Although by the eighteenth century – and probably long before – there was a deeply held tacit belief (and one made explicit in the Bill of Rights of 1689 and other laws) throughout virtually the whole of British society in the inalienable basic rights of the individual, there was, in contrast, certainly no such consensus about the extension of democratic political rights to the whole population until the twentieth century. On the contrary, until the later nineteenth century, such institutions of democratic government we now take for granted as universal adult suffrage, the secret ballot, and a severe limitation upon the powers of the hereditary House of Lords, were advocated only by a small minority of radicals. These democratic institutions were positively and vociferously opposed by most political activists and nearly everyone in the 'intelligentsia', as well as by all conservatives. The reasons for this hostility to a political system now both taken for granted and universally accepted throughout the Western world lie in the fear of the unknown, a deep mistrust of government by mob, and memories of the 'Reign of Terror' during the French Revolution. Prior to the late nineteenth century, few educated Englishmen would have thought it possible to combine an efficient, stable, and responsive government with an electorate in which the working class and the poor represented a majority of all voters.[4] This century's political reality in Britain, where universal adult suffrage has produced a Labour Party committed to socialism, yet willing (until now) to coexist with the traditional institutions of the monarchy, the House of Lords and the established Church, as well as maintain private property and law and order, would have struck most nineteenth-century observers as a bewildering impossibility. From Burke onwards, nearly all British conservatives warned that universal adult suffrage[5] would lead inevitably to mob rule and anarchy of the French Revolution pattern, doubtless followed by the rise of a demagogic dictator along the lines of Napoleon. Most nineteenth-century liberals, for instance Macaulay and John Stuart Mill, also opposed universal adult suffrage and wished the franchise restricted to the propertied and well educated. When extensions of the franchise to the working classes became a seriously argued proposition, much effort among liberals (and conservatives) went into the invention of franchise schemes which would give the well educated and propertied several votes to avoid the middle-class minority being 'swamped' by the propertyless majority. It is probably not generally realized today that the principle of 'one man (or woman), one vote' became a reality in Britain only in *1948*. Until then, a minority of the population was entitled to vote *more than once* at a General Election, including university graduates (for special university seats) and freemen of the City of London (for City of London seats), while well into the twentieth century anyone owning property in several constituencies could vote in each of these constituencies.[6] Until 1918, indeed, voting in Britain was not a right vested in all adult males at all, but given only to adult men who qualified to vote by virtue of residence in a place for a sufficient period of time, by the ownership of various forms of sufficient property or other means (such as graduation from a university). These qualifications varied from city (borough) to country (county) constituencies and between England and Wales, Scotland, and Ireland. Between 1832 and 1867 there were *thirty* such separate ways of qualifying to vote, of which the best known were the forty shilling freeholding requirement in English counties and the £10 householder qualification in English boroughs (Cook and Keith, 117–18).

Nevertheless, the franchise in Britain was gradually but inevitably extended to all adults in the century following 1832, to the skilled urban working class in 1867, to agricultural labourers in 1884, to all adult males and women over thirty in 1918, and to women aged 21–30 in 1928. A further reform in 1969 lowered the voting age to 18.

Perhaps just as important as the gradual democratization of the franchise was a concomitant evolution in the representativeness of Parliament, the increasing equalization (in terms of number of inhabitants) of Parliamentary seats. Prior to 1832 the unrepresentativeness of the boroughs entitled to send members to Parliament was proverbial and scandalous. Birmingham, Manchester, Leeds, Sheffield and most London boroughs were unrepresented in the House of Commons, while East Looe and West Looe in Cornwall, with one hundred electors between them, returned *four* MPs. Gatton (with *two* voters), Old Sarum (seven), Droitwich (with fourteen), and Camelford (twenty) likewise returned two MPs each. Six counties in northern Scotland returned a total of only three MPs, *taking turns* at returning at MP at every other election! Conservative defenders of the unreformed electoral system claimed that most 'interests' in the country were indeed represented in Parliament, since businessmen could often 'purchase' a seat in a small borough, but ultimately the absurdity of the old system became indefensible, and most of the very small boroughs were abolished. As with so much in nineteenth-century political reform, change was surprisingly gradual, and it was not until 1884–5 that Parliamentary seats were really roughly equal in size. In more recent times, although all seats are nearly equal in size, Scotland and

Wales have been overrepresented compared with England, possessing more seats per head of population, while Northern Ireland has been underrepresented. Parliamentary boundaries are also regularly altered every ten to fifteen years, to keep pace with the changing geographical distribution of the population. Until the First World War, these changes consistently and progressively increased the strength in Parliament of working-class and northern urban seats, which had hitherto been underrepresented; more recently, and increasingly, the processes of suburbanization and the depopulation of inner city seats have gradually increased the number of safe Tory seats at the expense of Labour. It was estimated that the Conservative Party added fifteen extra seats to its 1983 majority because of the boundary revisions carried out just before the election.

Mention of today's 'safe' Parliamentary seats reminds us that many contemporary critics of Parliament believe that, even now, the entire basis of Parliamentary elections is unequal and unjust in that the number of seats won by each party at an election is not proportionate to the respective number of votes cast. In particular, third parties, even those polling millions of votes, are systematically squeezed by the 'first past the post' system of elections. Additionally, the number of seats gained by the winning party is invariably inflated by the same electoral system.[7] Everywhere, and in every seat, votes cast for the losing candidates are simply wasted. Moreover, the geographical basis of the present Parliamentary system means that the winning party in 400 or more 'safe' seats is a virtual certainty and preordained: Labour is absolutely certain to win most inner city and mining seats, the Conservatives equally certain to win nearly all rural and middle-class suburban seats. A Labourite living in Surrey, or a Tory in Glasgow might literally pass an entire lifetime without ever being represented by a candidate of his choice. For all of these reasons, and others of a similar nature, many people now advocate some form of proportional representation by which parties would elect members to Parliament more proportionately to their overall vote. Calls for reform of the voting system have been greatly accentuated by the increase in the Liberal vote since the 1960s and, more recently, by the rise of the Social Democrats, who standing together as the Alliance won 26 per cent of the total vote at the 1983 General Election but elected only a derisory number of MPs. In response, critics of proportional representation point to the stability of the present system and to the instability of regimes, above all Weimar Germany, which adopted proportional representation, as well as to the certainty that it would lead to a multi-party system productive of weak, short-lived governments (as in Fourth Republic France) or one where extremists and special interest parties might gain excessive power (as in today's Israel).

Another major reason for the failure of Britain to institute proportional representation is the fact that the present political system seems to provide an advantage to both of the two major parties in that they and they alone – at least up till now – have been able to win an election and form a government. Reforming the electoral system in a basic way might well change this state of affairs. This points to another feature of the present system, namely that the big political parties organize and control the system – often, it seems, to the detriment of the 'ordinary' citizen. Critiques of this variety frequently claim that the big parties represent and are responsive to only the big interests they reflect – preeminently the trade unions on one side and the business class on the other – and are hence essentially undemocratic. Their beholdenness to big interests, it is claimed, has produced the widespread alienation from politics so noticeable in recent decades, with relatively lower turnouts at elections, less significant membership or participation in the party machinery or the political process, the growth of extremist movements at both ends of the spectrum, Celtic independence parties, and the great rise in the fortunes of the Liberal–SDP alternative. Some would argue, possibly reflecting an 'elitist' position (see pp. 17–18 above), that the big parties deliberately act to thwart 'populist' demands reflecting the deeply held but unacceptable views of the ordinary people, especially on those two most desired populistic changes which would probably pass any referendum by a large majority – restoring the death penalty and decreasing the size of the non-white population of Britain.

If this be true, it may be that the lack of pure democracy evident in the present British political system acts to preserve the values of liberalism and perhaps of liberty. From the viewpoint of equality and inequality, however, if the present system acts to entrench the so-called big interests, one may question whether the 'ordinary man' is more nearly equal than his predecessors in the past. And when governments respond at all to demands made by those outside of the interests traditionally served by the major parties, they generally do so only to the organized lobbying pressures of large groups of individuals. It is seemingly this inability of the individual meaningfully to influence the major policies of any government which has given rise to the considerable alienation from politics and politicians which is a marked feature of contemporary Britain. This feeling of helplessness is increased when it is realized that nearly all of the administrative and clerical work of the government and the services and duties it has legally enacted are carried out not by elected representatives but by permanent officials of the Civil Service, an organization formidable in size and privilege, opaque in its daily business, and notorious nearly everywhere in the modern world for red tape, secrecy, impersonality, misdirected profligacy and parsimony combined, administrative error and delay – attributes with which it is indeed virtually synonymous. Such a reputation widely attaches to Britain's civil service today, despite its long-standing good name for integrity and impartiality.

Although formal voting conditions may now be reasonably democratic (a proposition questioned by supporters of proportional representation), there still remain major institutions of British government from the time before democracy, most notably the monarchy and the House of Lords. The true powers and influence of the monarchy remain one of the few areas of the governance of contemporary Britain about which very little is known. Given the strictly confidential nature of the relationship between the sovereign and the prime minister, virtually nothing about the actual influence of the monarch upon the prime minister is likely to be known until many decades have elapsed, if ever. Although the sovereign has the constitutional right to be kept informed by her prime minister and to warn him or her, it is widely assumed that her powers have diminished to the merely symbolical. But the sovereign and the prime minister meet and discuss public affairs on at least a weekly basis, often over a period of five or ten years, and it may well be imagined that in a hundred ways both direct and subtle, the influence of the sovereign on policy is more than symbolic. This may well be greatly to the public good, and it is an undeniable fact that the monarchy is one of the few public institutions in Britain which is genuinely and almost universally popular, a popularity which seems, moreover, to increase with each decade.

The House of Lords has also diminished markedly in power and prestige over the past century, a diminution which was made official by its formal loss of powers to the Commons in 1911. Few well-informed political observers in 1911 could have imagined that the House of Lords would still survive in a virtually unreformed way nearly seventy-five years later, and its survival is an anomaly *par excellence* among contemporary legislatures. The Lords once consisted, almost exclusively, of great landowners, to whose number, especially between 1880 and 1945, were added dozens of leading businessmen, while most senior politicians have always received a peerage. Many life peers created in the last twenty-five years were drawn from 'the great and the good', those public worthies and notables, as well as retired politicians and political activists. The Lords probably owes its continued existence to two factors: its usefulness as a place of debate for superannuated politicians and other public notables, and, more importantly, the failure of the parties to agree on any scheme of reform or replacement for the Lords. Until recently no party wished to abolish the Lords outright, and any replacement for it would either make it more important – for instance, if it became an elected Senate on the American model – or would increase still further the patronage powers of the party leaders, if reform led to a wholly appointive upper house. Many traditionalist Conservatives, even now, would regret the gratuitous ending of a centuries-old institution, especially as most such root-and-branch reforms in Britain this century have never produced the benefits their advocates promise. Given the fact that seventy per cent of its membership still owe their places to heredity, however, the question of the Lords is likely to remain on the political agenda, albeit among the minor questions of the day.

This survey of political inequality has shown that the growth of democracy in a formal sense has been one of the major hallmarks of the past two hundred years. Despite this, democracy in modern Britain is based upon the existence of political parties widely perceived as responsive only to big interests and largely oblivious to the individual, and a realistic critique of political equality today may thus be quite different from that suggested by the formal tenets of the electoral system.

Social equality

As a concept, social equality is considerably more difficult for the historian to examine, or even to define, than either legal or political equality. The benchmarks in the area of legal and political equality are definite historical events – the adoption of the Bill of Rights, or the passage of the 1832 Reform Bill, for example – while many if not all of the major changes in the area of social equality represent changes in the perceived status of individuals and social groups, and are therefore much more difficult even to define precisely. By the evolution of 'social equality' we generally mean changes in the ascription of status or prestige to particular individuals or groups *as perceived by others*, and it is often particularly difficult to present an accurate chronology of change in this area. Accounts of the changes in the degree of prestige or status accorded to particular social groups – for instance, to lawyers or to industrialists – often vary from historian to historian, and there is really no agreed history of social status in modern Britain. Finally, it is often extremely difficult, if not impossible, to separate the social dimension – status, prestige, authority, deference, and the other concepts included in this concept – from the legal, political, or economic dimensions of social stratification. On the other hand, it should not be assumed that changes in the social status of groups need be congruent or even parallel with the evolution of the legal, political, or economic status of these groups, and they can, it would seem, move or evolve in different directions (although this may be a controversial view). For instance, the status of the landed aristocracy and of the landed ethos was still high after their political and economic decline had begun, while trade union leaders do not even today enjoy a high social status though often being politically very powerful.

Throughout modern British history, at least until the late nineteenth century, high status was very largely a function of the ownership of substantial amounts of land; the more land one owned, in general the higher social status one enjoyed. In particular, the ranks and orders in Britain's titled aristocracy as a rule varied with landed wealth, with dukes generally owning more land than marquesses and earls, who owned more than viscounts, barons, and baronets. Until the late nineteenth century, wealthy businessmen and leading professionals, when they were given a title at all, were almost never given a peerage but instead had to 'settle' for a knighthood. On the other hand, a sudden and rapid growth in the landed fortunes of an already titled landowner often led to an elevation in the peerage. For instance, successive heads of the Grosvenor family held only a baronetcy as late as 1761, but within just over a century were created Baron (1761) and Earl

Grosvenor (in 1784), Marquess of Westminster (1831) and in 1874 Duke of Westminster. In the meantime their lands in west central London, formerly virtually worthless, had been developed as Oxford Street, Mayfair, Pimlico, and Chelsea, and the Grosvenors had become the richest family in England. Somewhat similarly, the second Marquess of Stafford (1758–1833) married the Countess of Sutherland and inherited her land and then – talk about some people being born lucky! – inherited the Duke of Bridgewater's canals, and was created Duke of Sutherland shortly before his death. At his death he was certainly the wealthiest landowner in Britain, and his wealth was recognized with promotion to the highest rank in the peerage. Landed wealth remained the basis of high social status perhaps into the twentieth century, with most peerages created even in the latter part of the nineteenth century given to men with at least some land (Thompson, 292–300). Landed wealth, it was widely believed, possessed one quality which no business, regardless of how lucrative or well established it might seem to be, could ever possess: permanence. The land of Britain, barring only another Flood, would always be there. No business could ever claim this, and some firms which seemed to be as secure as the Rock of Gibraltar did go bankrupt or crash, as Baring Brothers, the great merchant bank, did in 1890. For any system of status based upon heredity and the inheritance of formal titles, the consideration of permanence remained highly important for a very long time. Beyond the actual ownership of land was the unwritten ethos of the English gentleman, closely modelled upon the code of the landed gentry, with its emphasis on duty, the absence of braggartry or demonstrativeness, little or no direct interest in business life, especially its seamier or more acquisitive side, 'noblesse oblige' toward one's social inferiors, sportsmanship, manliness, and a fairminded code of conduct toward one's social equals. This code was 'pre-industrial' in that it strongly suggested the conduct of courtly medieval knights and Crusaders, and was deliberately intended to contrast with the 'cash nexus', vulgar display, and Darwinian self-interest typical of the upstart 'self-made man' in the business world. This code, it is widely argued, was imparted to most of the upper middle classes by the new or reformed public schools of the nineteenth century (Honey, 47–103; Gathorne-Hardy, *passim*). Transferred to the business classes as the sons and grandsons of self-made Victorian businessmen became 'gentlemen', it is also widely argued that the code of the gentleman was among the main causes of Britain's post-1870 economic decline (Coleman, *passim*). Whatever the truth of this suggestion – which has been questioned by other historians – it is certainly widely believed that the code of conduct of the English gentleman was antagonistic to that of the businessman.

Some historians, indeed, for instance Martin Wiener, have gone further and argued that Britain's 'spirit' during the nineteenth century was quite antipathetic to entrepreneurship or to the more robust elements in business success (Wiener, *passim*). This may be disputed – there was a continuing ideology, whose most famous exponent was Samuel Smiles, which celebrated the 'self-made man' and the success of the individual entrepreneur – but it seems clear enough that high status continued to go with a landed lifestyle, in spirit if not in reality, into the twentieth century. However, it should be emphasized that in Britain, unlike continental Europe, businessmen were never regarded socially as utterly inferior to the aristocracy. Those businessmen who were more socially accept-able to the traditional aristocracy were, in general, London based bankers and merchants rather than northern industrialists, although the 'self-made man' continued to be received with a mixture of admiration and condescension (Rubinstein, 'Wealth Elites', 112–17).

Professional men enjoyed increasing prestige and status during the nineteenth century and some professions, most notably medicine, rose markedly in prestige and authority during the century (Reader, *passim*; Duman, *passim*; Haig, *passim*; Petersen, *passim*). Traditionally, the three accepted and prestigious professions were the (Anglican) clergy, law, and medicine, although most doctors, and solicitors among lawyers, were never as prestigious as barristers and clergymen. Barristers were close to the 'gentlemanly' ideal in a variety of ways: a client could deal with a barrister only through the intermediary of a solicitor (or, in the case of silks, through two intermediaries) and barristers could not sue for their fees. They wore a specialized, antique uniform and obeyed stringent rules of legal etiquette. The legal profession occupied a curious position. Judges and barristers have always enjoyed extremely high status, and many aristocratic sons were for centuries traditionally given a legal education at one of the Inns of Court. Lord Chancellors were always given a peerage (and still are) and many, like Lord Eldon, became large landowners. Solicitors, however, were regarded as of a socially inferior station prior to the nineteenth century. The nineteenth century saw something of an evening out of the two branches of the law, with solicitorship becoming more genteel and thoroughly professionalized, and barristers moving further from the world of the aristocracy and gentry than previously, although barristers continued to enjoy unquestioned prestige while it almost always required some independent income for an unknown young barrister to see himself through until his reputation was made. The nineteenth century also saw the 'professionalization' of many other occupations ranging from civil, mechanical, and electrical engineering to pharmacy to librarianship. The process of professionalization, which was fairly similar everywhere, entailed regularizing and governing entry into the profession by determining approved paths of apprenticeship, education, and examination, setting a scale of professional fees and salaries, restricting and eliminating outside practitioners from the profession, the establishment of a professional society, a professional journal, internal disciplinary procedures, and the like. The aim of professionalization was twofold: to give to the occupation a body of accepted knowledge which all future practitioners would have to learn in a prescribed way, and, plainly, to increase the fees and salaries of practitioners by restricting a monopoly of practice to those who served the approved apprenticeship, and only to them. The effect of deliberate professionalization upon each field was, generally, also to create an ethos and ambiance closer to the 'gentlemanly' ideal and less directly commercialized. The number of professional men greatly increased during the nineteenth century – barristers increased from 880 in 1810 to 3298 in 1850 – but (as is not generally appreciated) the largest single segment among professional men remained Anglican clergymen, who also expanded quite substantially, from 14,613 in 1841 to 25,363 in 1901 (Duman, 9; Haig, 3). Nevertheless, although the professional class grew substantially in size in the century following industrialization, it is arguable whether the middle classes as a whole increased relatively in size, compared with the entire British population, which grew at an unprecedented rate from about 1770 onwards. No precise or even imprecise figures exist, but it seems that, broadly, about 15–20 per cent of the entire adult male workforce was 'middle class' in some sense from before industrialization until the twentieth century. This figure is probably controversial, as much depends upon how one categorizes the occupational groups generally termed the 'lower middle class'.

Apart from the social differences between the landowners, businessmen, and professionals was the question of their wealth and incomes. Since this topic will be discussed in more detail later, it need only be said here that social status varied in at least a rough way with income and wealth, although it was by no means the only determinant of prestige. Not only occupation (as in the case of landowners *vis-à-vis* industrialists), but such factors as religion (Anglicans *vis-à-vis* dissenters and others), region and residence (the south of England and rural areas were always more prestigious than industrial cities and the north) and the 'newness' of one's family (with long lineage more prestigious, in general, than a recent origin), were all significant in determining status among 'elite' groups and the middle class. Even so, it is perhaps not sufficiently well realized that the richest landowners remained the richest men in Britain until the twentieth century, while the number of very wealthy businessmen was far smaller than the number of wealthy landowners until the end of the nineteenth century.

The great divide in the nineteenth-century British status structure was (and remains) that between the middle classes (and above) and the working classes, although the status of the intermediate lower middle class of clerks, small shopkeepers, tradesmen, shop assistants, minor bureaucrats and the like has always been ambiguous. Historically, the lower middle class was extremely keen to differentiate itself from the working classes, by such means of nineteenth-century self-identification as the wearing of middle-class clothing, living in specifically class-defined areas of cities, seeking respectability and maintaining an image often characterized as one of 'shabby gentility', although lower-middle-class groups in Britain seldom formed occupational protection associations as on the continent (Crossick, 41–6; Offer, 101–4). To most lower-middle-class men and families – apart from those in 'safe' government careers – the great fear was losing one's job or source of income and being forced into the working class. To such lower-middle-class groups, it seems clear that the status effects of unemployment and impoverishment outweighed even their economic effects.

It goes without saying that, throughout history, working-class groups were of a lower status than middle-class ones, although it has been frequently argued that their status declined still further after industrialization, since the gap in income and wealth between the rich and the poor probably widened. (There is a discussion of this in the next section.) Within the working class, there were increasing differentiations between skilled labourers with sufficient income and security of tenure to escape from poverty – often belonging to the so-called 'aristocracy of labour' – and the unskilled or those in occupations which were increasingly mechanized out of existence by industrialization, of whom the handloom weavers are the most celebrated example. To the unskilled factory workers must also be added the agricultural labourers, in the nineteenth century generally the lowest paid of all occupations in which adult males predominated. It will be seen that the defining characteristics of high and low status for the working classes as well as the middle classes were a combination of income and other factors. Income and wealth was generally central to the status and prestige of an occupational or social group, but was by no means the only criterion in the common perceptions of the status of any group.

The twentieth century has seen a number of important modifications of the traditional British status system. Most significantly, the historical ascendancy of the landed and titled aristocracy has been greatly reduced if not entirely disappeared. Though there is, of course, still an aristocracy with new annual creations of peers and knights, the criteria for ennoblement have been vastly broadened to include trade union leaders, nearly all senior politicians including Labour politicians, entertainment figures, sporting notables, and persons of literary and cultural prominence. At the same time the political significance of the traditional landed aristocracy has greatly diminished, while their traditional way of life has largely disappeared. So antiquated does the traditional status system now seem that sociologists concerned to measure prestige through surveys of public attitudes on social status seldom if ever attempt to gauge the position of these traditional elite groups in the contemporary status hierarchy; indeed, the thought of so doing would possibly strike many sociologists as bizarre.

Instead, contemporary sociologists concerned with measuring the prestige of occupations and groups in contemporary Britain have discovered that the hierarchy of occupations is remarkably similar here to other countries around the world (Abrahamson, Mizruchi, and Hornburg, 193–6). In such occupational rankings, physicians, judges, academics and higher public officials are invariably regarded as more prestigious than most businessmen, with other white-collar and middle-class occupations more prestigious than working-class occupations and unskilled trades, especially those associated with unpleasant tasks (such as refuse collections) at the bottom of the social hierarchy. There is thus a correlation between income and perceived social prestige, although seldom if ever is a working–class trade accorded a higher status in the eyes of a random sample of the general public than a white-collar occupation, regardless of their respective incomes, even if – as is not un-common today – some working-class trades actually earn more than some white-collar positions. At the top end of the social hierarchy, there is much less of a correlation between income and prestige, and, in particular, there is much less of a correlation between wealth (as opposed to income) and prestige. Instead, occupations which are commonly deemed to be necessary or socially worthy and estimable (such as a physician), which are middle class and require a considerable degree of training and skill (such as a lawyer) or which require knowledge and (it is perceived) unusual intelligence (such as an academic), are regarded as more socially prestigious than other occupations. Physicians, and especially surgeons, are always ranked as the most prestigious occupation because surgeons are at once socially supremely worthy, require great skilfulness, and equally great learning. Additionally, occu-pations or categories which are seen to be politically or socially powerful (such as Members of Parliament) are also highly pres-tigious. Physicians, who have the power to prolong life, and judges, who can free or imprison, are again invariably seen as enjoying the highest prestige of all. Although the earning of a high income counts for a good deal in the popular assessment of social prestige, at the very top of the social hierarchy income or wealth is evidently not as important as any of the qualities we have noted, or else bankers, company directors and major landowners would be ranked above many or most doctors and lawyers, and certainly above academics. This ranking of the occupational hierarchy, moreover, has been found to be almost identical in random public opinion surveys carried out not merely in most Western countries, but in several non-Western and Third World nations as well, and suggests that there is a near universal value system of occupational prestige which is anything but traditional and pre-modern.

This ubiquitous occupational hierarchy, it seems, closely

approximates to that which should exist in the functionalist theory of social stratifications discussed above (pp. 18–19). Prestige as well as more tangible income rewards are accorded to the most socially necessary and responsible occupations, or to those which require the most skill, education, or learning. To be sure, in the popular mind these standards are not universally applied, or working-class trades such as craftsmen or electricians which also require considerable skill and responsibility would be popularly accorded higher status than most middle-class occupations which do not require these characteristics. This would indicate either that white-class status *per se* or a higher income *per se* imply higher social prestige or status in the popular mind, and no doubt the popular perceptions of prestige are sufficiently complicated or confused to be a mixture of several ingredients. Nevertheless, it is equally striking that great wealth or a high income alone certainly does not automatically confer equally high prestige.

There are, of course, no opinion surveys about social prestige in Britain prior to the past few decades, and we have no equivalent rankings of social prestige from the last century. Nevertheless, it seems clear that the popular perception of high social prestige in Britain during the past century or more has changed considerably, with the traditional landed and titled leaders of society, once unequivocally at the top of the social hierarchy, giving way to new social elites whose place, it would seem, is owed to more 'rational' determinants of prestige. Unfortunately, it is very difficult to determine when this transformation occurred, although it is likely that it was a drawn-out process lasting from the mid-Victorian period until the Second World War.

It is equally difficult to be certain about this, but it would also seem at least plausible that there has been a narrowing of the gap in prestige between the highest and lowest groups, for a number of reasons. There is, as we have seen, at least a rough association between income and social status, and income differentials in Britain have narrowed since the First World War and especially during the past twenty-five years. More importantly, no political power or wider power in the general community flows *per se* from membership in those groups like doctors and lawyers which enjoy the highest prestige (although the active doctors' and lawyers' lobbies are certainly politically significant). On the contrary, some working-class groups like the leadership of the key trade unions may be popularly regarded as more politically powerful in contemporary Britain than high prestige middle-class groups. There may thus well be no perceived overlap between power and status in the case of today's high prestige groups as there was in the case of landed aristocrats before the twentieth century or even urban factory owners – who often served as local JPs, civic officials, and members of Parliament in industrial areas – during the nineteenth century. Today, doctors, scientists, and academics are deferred to (if indeed they are) not because they represent a traditional elite but because they are thought by most laymen to have acquired specialized knowledge of a high order not possessed by the average man. If we grant that the reason why groups like doctors and academics enjoy high prestige is because of a generalized 'functionalist' view of their role in society, then the ascription of high prestige to these groups is because of a 'rational' value system in which socially valuable and highly educated members of society enjoy the most prestige, and it may well follow that such a value system stands in contrast to 'pre-modern' societal value systems in which high prestige is accorded to traditional and hereditary leaders of society while, in modern liberal society, lower prestige is accorded to most ordinary people; it is difficult to believe that modernity and contemporary life have not narrowed the gap, in the popular mind, between the rich and powerful on the one hand and the poor on the other. This would simply accord with the narrowing between the elite and the rest which is seemingly a ubiquitous feature of twentieth-century Western societies. Such a narrowing of status may well be reflected in other ways, such as the similarity of dress and consumption patterns among a wide portion of the British population.

One may, indeed, question whether the notions of prestige and social status have any real pragmatic significance in the modern world. The days when a significant section of the rural population, or even urban factory workers (Joyce, 90–133), deferred to their local landowners or factory owners certainly ended with the First World War, and in today's Britain it is difficult to believe that this type of deference exists in any shape or form, except possibly in the glow surrounding the Royal Family and in the etiquette and enforced ritual of the law courts. Since new groups entirely outside the traditional status system are widely believed to enjoy high prestige in the eyes of specific subcultures – pop groups to many teenagers is an often cited example – the notion may now be more confusing than helpful. The disintegration of the simple certainties of the traditional British status system has indeed left much status confusion in its wake, with Labour (working-class) governments and prime ministers, the House of Lords packed with life peers more socially valuable than wealthy or aristocratic, and the rise of 'celebrities', stars, and current heroes. Margaret Thatcher, a woman, the daughter of a provincial grocer, grammar school educated, yet a right-wing Tory and the master (mistress?) of aristocrats, millionaires, old Etonians, and grouse moor landowners in her party, herself well illustrates the mixed and contradictory signals which attach to prestige in contemporary Britain.

With the evolution of social equality, it is often particularly difficult to separate the historical chicken from the historical egg, that is, whether widespread changes in status perceptions are caused by other changes, possibly political or economic in nature, or whether changes in status perception cause these shifts in other spheres. For instance, were women granted the vote in 1918 because of perceived changes in their social status, as a result, say, of the First World War, or did changes in their economic functions and political status lead to a widespread change in their perceived social status and prestige? This is a particularly difficult area to unravel, and the evidence is contradictory: the British working class did not suddenly or basically rise in prestige upon being granted the vote in 1867; on the other hand, votes were granted to them, historians are generally agreed, as a kind of 'reward' for twenty years of social and political class peace in Britain following the agitation of the Chartist and Corn Law repeal periods of the 1840s, and it is quite possible that the popular image of the British working class changed in this period; from the point of view of the middle classes and indeed part of the working classes themselves, it may have 'improved'.

Economic equality

Since most of this book is concerned with the evolution of equality and inequality in the economic sphere in Britain, our discussion of it here will be briefer than for the other forms of equality discussed above. The concept of economic equality and inequality seems to differ from the other three concepts of equality we have examined in a number of key respects. In the first place, the concept itself appears to have the paradoxical feature of being at once less easy to define precisely or clearly in a way which would attract general agreement, while at the same time referring specifically to the holding by individuals of highly quantifiable attributes or possessions such as income, wealth, purchasing power, consumer goods, and the like. Secondly, in our society and in most others, in practice many aspects of one's economic status represent the inheritance of money or goods from one's parents or other relatives or the 'start in life' provided by them through the economic advantages they enjoyed; in contrast, in the twentieth century, the right to vote or to freely express oneself is not inherited in this way but accords to all adults by virtue of living in a democracy. One's economic status, too, is generally bound up with one's immediate family; in the case of such groups as married women and children outside the labour force, economic status seems to be wholly dependent upon the income enjoyed by the family breadwinner and is normally perceived in terms of his income or occupation.

More importantly, perhaps, while in the twentieth century there has been a near universal consensus in British society and amongst its intelligentsia that legal and political equality are unquestionably necessary and hence desirable features of a democratic society, and also much agreement that old fashioned pre-modern social delineations of rank and prestige are antiquated, there is much less consensus on the desirability of economic equality. Indeed, although everyone in contemporary British society except a few extremists and eccentrics would presumably agree that universal adult suffrage – one adult, one vote – is a desirable and necessary feature of British society, virtually no one believes in the *strict* equality of income and wealth. Only a handful of societies in the modern world, most notably China during the 'Cultural Revolution' and Kampuchea under Pol Pot, have ever attempted to enact and enforce the absolute equality of income and wealth, and their example hardly inspires confidence that such a goal is achievable in this world, let alone desirable.

In so far as a consensus does exist in contemporary Britain about what might be termed economic equality, it consists in basic agreement that a minimum standard of living should exist and be maintained by the state below which no individual may, theoretically, fall. Although this may strongly imply acceptance of the mechanisms of the modern Welfare State, it is probably true that at no time in British history did such a consensus *not* exist, nor was there a time when such a minimum standard did not exist in *some* form. The nineteenth-century workhouse and the rigorous legislative attempts to exclude 'outdoor relief' for the poor may strike all of us today as impossibly harsh, but these, too, were sincere attempts to create an absolute minimum standard of existence for the destitute sufficient to keep industrial England's poor from dying of starvation.

Beyond a consensus on such a minimum, however, there is no agreement whatever in contemporary Britain on what degree of economic equality ought to be enforced by the instrumentalities of the state, especially by the taxation system. As we have noted, the 'left' in Britain and elsewhere in the Western world is virtually defined by its commitment to greater equality of individual income and wealth and to greater state control of business activity in the interest of the 'general good', while the 'right' is equally often defined by its belief that individuals ought to be entitled to keep as much of their income and wealth as is consistent with maintaining the necessary functions of the state. To the left's interest in equity and social justice, the right posits a belief in economic efficiency and innovation as justifying economic inequality, while many Conservatives would in fact deny that what the left terms 'social justice' is just. Somewhere in the middle lie those proponents of Welfare State capitalism who would see the state's primary role as creating an ever-larger cake in the private sphere, from which a larger and innovative public sector would be funded. Although these ideological differences have always existed, they have probably become more pronounced during the past ten or fifteen years, with the collapse of the post-war Welfare State consensus and the movement of both the Conservative and Labour Parties to more extreme positions.

In the following chapter the historical evidence concerning the distribution of income and wealth in Britain during the past few centuries will be presented and analysed, and some of the implications of this evidence for questions of economic equality described. This analysis comprises the bulk of the material in this book, and is mainly that of an economic and social historian. For this reason, although abstract questions of morality and equity are addressed, the thrust is very much on ascertaining the main historical facts and trends of economic inequality and equality in modern British history.

II

The historical development of income and wealth distribution in Britain

Introduction

In the discussion in the earlier part of this book about the historical growth of equality in Britain, we asserted that trends in the economic sphere were by far the most difficult to measure and the area in which there exists the least general agreement. In this and the following chapters of the book, the historical evidence which does exist will be set out and examined. Although the basic questions we are asking are fairly straightforward, no discussion of them can proceed without reference to scholarly investigations of the subject which often necessarily entail some statistical evidence and some sophisticated numeracy.

The broader question of the historical evolution of economic equality in Britain might be subdivided into four subjects. The first two – the evolution of income distribution and the evolution of wealth distribution – are complex matters which require not only separate discussions, but an examination of the various factors which have led to today's reality. The question of changes in wealth distribution also includes the somewhat separate question of changes in living standards in terms of the ownership of houses and consumer durables. The two remaining aspects of this subject – the ownership and control of capital and the means of production and individual economic and social opportunities – will be discussed somewhat more briefly.

Some economic terms

In turning in some detail directly to the question of economic inequality, it is useful to address what we mean by some key economic terms, especially what is meant by 'income' and 'wealth', and how economic inequality is measured. One economics dictionary defines 'income' as 'the flow of money or goods accruing to an individual, group of individuals, a firm or the economy over some time period', and adds income 'may originate from the sale of productive services' – as wages, profits, interest, or rent – from a gift (such as an inheritance), a transfer payment via social security, or a payment 'in kind'. In traditional societies payment 'in kind' included the receipt of livestock or other agricultural produce; today it comprehends such things as executive fringe benefits like the use of a company car.

For the purposes of this discussion, several points in the above definition require some clarification. The relevant basic unit of time over which an income is received in this study, and in nearly all other studies which discuss economic inequality, is invariably one year. We are always concerned here with individual incomes, or, occasionally, family incomes, but never with the incomes of larger groups or units. The economic analysis of income distribution is always concerned with money incomes, such as wages, salaries, profits, and rents. Gifts, including inheritances, are included in statistics of income distribution only if they are registered or recorded by an individual statistician or by a governmental body (such as the Inland Revenue) concerned with establishing individual incomes; otherwise they go unrecorded. Similarly, transfer payments are generally recorded, but in many statistical computations they are not. Finally, income 'in kind' is hardly ever recorded; in the case of fringe benefits it is safe to say they are almost never recorded, except by economists who have attempted to make a special study of the subject. British income statistics in this century almost always derive from taxation statistics, and the untaxed and unrecorded 'black economy' is, by definition, not accounted for. Each of these factors affects the overall pattern of income distribution in a different way: some affect the validity of statistics about the rich, some, the poor. The reader might wish to think about how each type of omission is likely to change the overall picture derived from the statistics.

As with 'income', the definition of 'wealth' has a meaning to economists which must be carefully examined. The same economics dictionary defines the wealth of an individual as 'his total stock of tangible or intangible possessions which have a market value', and notes that 'this implies that they must be capable of being exchanged for money or other goods'. It should be carefully noted that wealth is, generally, accumulated income. Every person, or virtually every person, has an income of some kind, but not everyone possesses 'wealth', especially 'tangible or intangible possessions which have a market value'. If I earn relatively little and, for whatever reason, am unable to save virtually anything, I may well own no 'wealth' at all. Naturally, I will possess some personal chattels and possessions – my clothing, some furniture, utensils, and so on – but the market value of these may well be close to zero. For most people the most valuable piece of property they will ever own is their house, followed, a distant second, by their car, and the 'wealth' owned by most people consists of their house, their car, their savings, and whatever other marketable property they may possess. Property ownership and the ownership of 'wealth' in the sense normally connoted by these terms is confined in most Western societies to a small minority of persons who own substantial amounts of a business, stocks and shares, valuable possessions like rare paintings, and the like. The percentage of persons owning 'wealth' in this sense is, and, still more, was, microscopically small, as this book will make clear.

Income statistics are invariably measured in terms of the cash income (plus transfer payments) received by an individual (or family) in one particular year. This is not as clear-cut as it seems – some types of income, as noted above, are excluded, while in the contemporary world high levels of direct taxation produce a big difference between the gross and net incomes of individuals – but, generally, the measurement of income is fairly straightforward, as are the statistical sources from which these measurements derive – nearly always taxation statistics. The measurement of wealth, however, is far from simple. Since the nineteenth century, the most important (indeed virtually the only) consistent statistical source for the private ownership of wealth in Britain (and elsewhere in the Western world) are the probate statistics of wealth left at death. From this source the measurable wealth or property held by all persons deceased in a particular year are totalled according to their value on the day of death, but not during their lifetime prior to death.

Because wealth passing at death is taxed,[1] very complete data on the number of persons leaving taxable wealth at death and the amount of their legacies is available from the late nineteenth century onwards. Less complete data is available from an earlier period, while complete records of the names and value of the estate of anyone leaving property at death are available from the late eighteenth or early nineteenth centuries, although no tables of the total number of such persons and their property were drawn up and these early estate valuations exclude real (i.e. landed) property as well as some settled property.

Pictures of the distribution of wealth in Britain have frequently been compiled by economists from these probate statistics throughout this century, the key assumptions being that a portrait of private wealth left at death in a particular year mirrors that held by all living persons, and that changes in the distribution of this wealth over time reflect similar changes among the total population. Before examining how these measurements of wealth distributions are calculated, it is worth mentioning some of the more significant failings of this method of calculating inequality.[2] One of the most striking facts about the probate statistics is that, even today, about half of the adult population deceased in a particular year leaves *nothing*, while during the nineteenth century (as is made clear later on) the great majority of deceased adults left nothing. This has been the case because 'wealth', according to those who calculate these statistics, excludes persons who leave only very small amounts of property (currently £1500), as well as property not requiring a legal deed or title to pass to the heirs of the deceased (like furniture). In practice, too, the property of many deceased working-class persons has been outside of the probate net with its legal prerequisites and complications. Secondly, even among personal possessions which would certainly constitute 'wealth', some forms of property are omitted from the valuations of deceased estates, notably settled property over which the deceased had no absolute control and most pension rights. Thirdly, the valuations arrived at by the Inland Revenue in assessing the wealth left by probate are often, necessarily, arbitrary, though they are supposed to reflect market values at the day of death. The likely market value of a house or the resale value of an automobile is often, of course, a matter of opinion. Finally, there is the important matter of *inter vivos* gifts (that is, the giving away of one's property – generally to relatives – prior to death) and deliberate estate duty avoidance. Estates left by millionaires in Britain are currently taxed at 75 per cent and were, between 1949 and 1972, taxed at 80 or 85 per cent, while even fairly moderate estates are taxed at 30 per cent or more.

Maximum rates of duty on millionaire estates had already reached 15 per cent in 1904–14 and 50 per cent (on estates over £2 million) by 1930. It may well be imagined that some, and probably many, wealthy elderly persons would give away most of their property long before their death to their close relatives in order to avoid taxes of this magnitude. For this reason, death duties are often referred to as a 'voluntary tax' which few of the very wealthy actually pay, and the resulting inaccuracy of the statistics of the rich – if the statistics are indeed inaccurate – must sharply distort the overall statistics of inequality.

On the other hand, it must be noted that even for the very wealthiest, the probate statistics are probably not as inaccurate, even today, as might be imagined in advance. Since the mid-nineteenth century, taxes have been levied on *inter vivos* gifts made some years prior to the death of a wealth leaver in order to catch such 'deathbed' legacies. This period of time has gradually been increased. Many wealthy persons are extremely reluctant to entrust their property to anyone besides themselves, and the whole process appears far more complex than one might think. The number of very large estates is increasing very rapidly, not diminishing.[3] The largest British estate of the post-war period amounted to not less than £52.2 million, and was left by Sir John Ellerman, 2nd Bt, the shipping magnate, in 1973. In the five years between mid-1979 (when my list in *Men of Property* ends) and mid-1984, there have been fifteen estates of £5 million or more, headed by two estates of over £20 million. The largest of these estates – over £28 million – was left by Sir Charles Clore, the financier, who certainly had every opportunity and incentive to give away the bulk of his fortune prior to his death.[4]

It will thus be seen that the most important of these omissions in the comprehensiveness of the probate records pull, as it were, in different directions – the exclusion of half and more of the working class makes for an underestimation of property owned by the poor, while estate duty avoidance leads to an underestimation of total property owned by the rich.

From the viewpoint of the historian, however, none of these sources of error in the probate records is arguably as important as another which has, so far as I am aware, attracted little or no attention in the voluminous writing on this subject, namely that the probate valuations are highly *age specific to the elderly*, since they record only the wealth of recently deceased persons. The average age of such persons is not merely now well over seventy, but is actually somewhat higher than the median British lifespan, since virtually no deceased minors own any property. Although the age-specific nature of the probate statistics has various consequences which have been taken into account by many economists, from the point of view of the historical evolution of wealth distribution in Britain, they have one major facet which, it would seem, has been ignored: they reflect the patterns of social mobility and of the possibilities of wealth accumulation of two generations before. If the current average age of death of persons leaving property recorded in the probate statistics is, say, nearly eighty, this means that they completed their education and began their working careers in many cases over sixty years ago. In a society where individual opportunity and the opportunities to accumulate property and wealth are arguably widening constantly and, moreover, widening at an ever increasing rate, these increased opportunities would be reflected at best only partially, if at all, in the probate statistics, while the result of the social transformation of modern Britain, especially the opportunities arising from the ever increasing range of secondary and tertiary education, would be seen in these statistics hardly at all.

For this reason (as well as those others outlined above) studies of inequality in contemporary Britain which claim, for example, that at the present time the wealthiest ten per cent of the population owns seventy per cent of wealth in private hands, are seriously misleading if taken at face value: it would perhaps be more true to say that this mirrors the social opportunities not of the 1980s but of the 1920s and 1930s. Conversely, a much fairer test of wealth distribution would be accurately to assess the property owned by a statistically significant random sample of households, rather than to draw inferences from the probate statistics. Moreover, if likely *future* trends are sought, a fairer test still would be to assess wealth distribution among the *youngest* adult age cohorts (say aged 18–40) rather than, in effect, the oldest. Basing an overall national picture of wealth distribution on the estates left by persons on average in their mid-seventies has yet another distorting effect upon the likely accuracy of the statistics. Retired persons, such as the recently deceased generally are, by definition do not work and thus do not receive a wage or a salary in the normal sense. (We are ignoring here the fact that half of all deaths are those of women.) Most retirees receive pensions, generally rather minimal ones, and because of this, many retirees must live at least in part on the income from their accumulated savings or upon the capital resulting from the sale of assets (if any exist). The total wealth of these pensioners is thus continuously *shrinking*, and this process is augmented by *inter vivos* gifts and the extraordinary expenses which accompany old age. But another class of retirees, the wealthier kind, have assets which produce income greater than their expenditure. Their wealth is continuously *rising*. Once persons formerly in the labour force retire, and in the absence of opportunities to earn an additional income, the gap between the wealthier and poorer pensioners is thus continuously widening, almost certainly at a faster rate than among younger, employed persons in the labour force. As the average lifespan increases, this gap will very likely continuously grow.

There are many other respects in which a measurement of wealth distribution based on the probate statistics is inadequate. The probate valuations measure *individual* wealth, not family or *household* wealth or assets, and this further distorts the findings. The average lifespan has grown continuously over the past century, influencing the basis of the statistics. Pension rights and entitlements have, until recently, not been counted with the figures. Although undertaken by trained government valuers, the valuation of assets at death is necessarily arbitrary and (as in the case of the value of real estate or of such commodities as rare stamps and valuable paintings) entails a certain amount of guess work – and so on. Economists and historians who work with the probate statistics to produce data on wealth distribution in Britain are, of course, aware of these factors and attempt to make allowances for them. For instance, economists have evolved a fairly sophisticated methodology of varying mortality rates by social class. According to this procedure, the number of persons deceased at each age, and the total wealth left by them, is 'blown up' into a total societal picture by a 'mortality multiplier' (the inverse of the percentage of each age cohort deceased in a year). Doing this should identify *all* of the private wealth in society, yet most such studies have found a considerable shortfall in the total national wealth thus identified, compared with other independent studies of total private wealth based on other sources. It is likely that most of these sources of error in the probate figures *overstate* the amount of wealth inequality which actually exists in society. Despite all this, in the absence of searching and statistically significant random household samples of personal wealth, there is nothing better than the probate statistics, and the merits of this series ought not to be ignored. Among these is the fact that this series has existed for a very long period, and historical trends may be measured, the comprehensive (*all* deaths), independent and official nature of these statistics, and the rare picture which emerges, however half-true, of the very rich and the scale of their assets. For these reasons, they remain of lasting value to the researcher in this field.

What precisely is surveyed in these studies of income and wealth inequality? These studies survey the extent to which income or wealth is distributed equally or unequally. There are a number of statistical measurements which are commonly used to analyse wealth and income equality. One, termed the Gini coefficient after its discoverer, is briefly touched upon on p. 66. Another common device is to show what percentage of the total income or wealth is owned by the richest fraction or fractions of the whole population, by the next richest fraction, and so on down to the poorest. The following table (which also appears in a more detailed form in Table 9, p. 95) is a fair sample of the kind of survey of income and wealth distribution which may be found repeatedly in recent discussions of this subject. It shows the distribution of wealth among various portions of the adult British population at three different dates – 1936, 1960 and 1973.

TABLE 1: Distribution of wealth in Britain, 1936–73, by percentages[5]

Proportion of adults	1936	1960	1973
Top 1%	53.0%	35.1%	27.4%
Top 5%	77.0%	60.9%	51.9%
Top 10%	86.0%	73.4%	64.1%
Top 20%	92.2%	85.0%	n.a.
Bottom 80%	7.8%	15.0%	n.a.

'n.a.' = not available

This table shows that in 1936, the richest 1 per cent of the adult population owned 53.0 per cent of total British wealth. In 1960, the richest 1 per cent owned 35.1 per cent, while in 1973 the richest

1 per cent owned 27.4 per cent of all wealth. Naturally, the particular *individuals* in these three groups would be quite different at the three dates, with many of the 1936 rich dying by 1960 or 1973, new self-made men coming into the latter groups, etc. What remains constant between the three dates may be better grasped in this way: imagine a village consisting of exactly 1000 adults and with a distribution of wealth similar to that in the above table. If we arranged them, as it were, in a row from the richest to the poorest, the top 1 per cent of these villagers – that is, ten persons – would have owned 53.0 per cent of the total wealth of the village in 1936. We can imagine that this group of ten would include the local squire, a rich widow, the town's doctor and solicitor, a business-man or two who lived there, and others of this sort. If we went back to the village in 1960 – which still had a population of exactly 1000 – some of the 1936 individuals would have died or moved, new people settled there, children grown up, and so on – but the ten wealthiest persons could still be identified. These ten owned considerably less of the village's overall wealth than did the ten richest of 1936. We can imagine, say, that the squire had died and his son had to pay huge death duties, that the richest businessman was now on a salary rather than owning the assets of his company, that the solicitor now had increased competition. Similarly it appears that the ordinary villagers – the 990 *not* among the ten wealthiest – had become rather more prosperous, with many more now owning their own home, a car, and some bank savings, and other assets which might be termed 'wealth' in the sense such studies imply. It should also be noted that there were probably very considerable degrees of wealth inequality among even the top 1 per cent, with the squire (say) worth hundreds of thousands, many times more than the rich widow.

If we extend this picture to a national scale, we can readily grasp the information which Table 1, and others like it, attempt to convey. The top 1 per cent of British adults dying in 1936, out of a total of about 300,000 such persons, owned 53.0 per cent of all wealth. By 1960, the richest 1 per cent of adults (a larger number, given the rise in population) owned only 35.1 per cent of all wealth. By 1973, the richest 1 per cent owned only 27.4 per cent of all wealth. Clearly, the overall trend is for greater and greater equality, although it is equally notable that gross inequalities in wealth distribution continued to exist into the 1970s and the decline in the

proportion of total assets owned by the very rich has not necessarily meant that the poor own proportionately much more.

Although figures such as those in Table 1 are often quoted by
commentators on the distribution of wealth and power in society,
as lengthy and important a list can be drawn up of what such
statistics do *not* say. What they do *not* indicate or suggest is at least
as important as what they do. It is worth making a few of the more
important points about what these indices of wealth and income
inequality do not tell us:
– They do not tell us anything about the absolute amount of
income earned or wealth owned by the very rich, or, indeed, about
anyone else. The richest 1 per cent may be multi-millionaires or
may be worth considerably less, depending upon the society, the
date of the survey, and the indices used. The poorest 30 per cent of
today would be unimaginably wealthy compared to their equivalent in Dickens' time.
– Similarly, they tell us nothing about the general degree of
affluence in society or the average standard of living. There is a
considerable difference between living in a society where wealth is
rather unequally distributed, but where the average man enjoys
some degree of affluence, and a society where there is general and
widespread poverty.

In fact it is *most important* to keep in mind that the average
standard of living and these statistics of wealth and income distribution are absolutely independent of one another.

It is probably true, as we shall see, that in twentieth-century
Britain there has been ever increasing income and wealth distribution
together with the growth of an 'affluent society', but it is certainly
not necessarily true that these two developments are causally
connected. Similarly (but separately) there are societies like the
United States where the rich mainly avoid taxes and probably are
far wealthier than are the wealthy in Britain, but where the average
income and standard of living are higher than in Britain.
– These statistics tell us little or nothing about the amount of
poverty in Britain, although at first glance it may seem as if they
do. Even if the poorest 80 per cent still own or earn only a small
percentage of the overall cake, it could well be that many or most
of them earn more than an income associated with poverty. As
national wealth has grown in modern times, so have working-class
incomes and the general ownership of property. In any historical

study of this topic, in particular, it is important to keep squarely in mind the steady rise in *per capita* income and the decline in primary poverty, which may be quite separate from any long-term trend toward wealth and income equalization.

These figures tell us nothing whatever about many areas of power and control in society, for instance the power held and exercised by the Labour (or Conservative) Party when in office, by trade unions (or industry), by lobbies and interests of various kinds, by the media, and so on.

Similarly, they tell us nothing whatever about any other economic indicator or factor at work in shaping British society – inflation, taxation, unemployment, labour relations, the balance of trade, government economic policy, overseas trade, the value of the pound sterling, or economic growth rates. These factors may or may not influence the distribution of wealth and income, but nothing about them may be inferred simply from the statistics of wealth and income inequality.

Finally, the fact that these statistics are expressed in the form of precise numerical data lends them a semi-spurious exactitude, and conceals the ambiguities inherent in the broader figures on which they are based, in the definition of what is to be measured, in the accuracy of the data collection, in the interpretations to be placed on them, and in many other aspects of this topic which have been or will be discussed. A historical study of this subject will reveal broad trends which are probably accurate, but there is most certainly a wide margin of error in any 'snapshot' examination of income and wealth distribution at a particular time. This is probably more the case with this subject than with many others in economic history.

Of the points made here, probably the most important are the second and the third. Indices of wealth and income *distribution* are irrelevant to understanding either the overall degree of affluence or the per capita income of a society. It is my belief that average standards of living, including such things as home ownership, ownership of consumer durables, and household savings among typical family units are a more important guide to the economic development of a society than are wealth or income distribution. Following from this, those social critics who use the statistics of wealth and income distribution to demonstrate the continuing unsatisfactory circumstances of the poor even in today's supposedly affluent society are in danger of misusing these statistics, which tell us nothing about the actual wealth or income enjoyed by the poor (or anyone else) and certainly cannot tell us anything at all as to how disadvantaged today's poor are compared with their equivalents in the past. It is wisest that the historian treat these statistics (and others, for that matter) with the caution they deserve.

No historian who has worked closely with this data can fail to realize how inexact and imprecise the figures for individual income and wealth were prior to this century, nor – as will become apparent in the next chapter – how glaring are the omissions and gaps at critical stages of Britain's development. Nevertheless broad historical trends are discernible, and our knowledge becomes much more certain as we approach the present.

The distribution of income in Britain since 1695

Speaking in broad historical terms, and ignoring the many short-term nuances of change, three views* of the overall distribution of wealth and income in British society from early modern times to the present have been put. These are

  – the view that income and wealth have become more and more concentrated since the pre-industrial era, i.e., that wealth and income are increasingly concentrated in fewer and fewer hands;

  – the view that levels of inequality *rose* during industrialization and then *fell* during the post-industrial period;

  – the view that income and wealth have become progressively more equally divided since industrialization.

Each of these views is a broad historical perspective and is relevant to long-term rather than short-term trends. Income distribution might (say) have become more unequal for a period of five or even ten years at any past time, but then continued, for a much longer time, to become more equally distributed. Probably it is best to view these very general perspectives as generational; that is, they describe trends which are fully perceptible only if income distri-

---

*A fourth view, that income distribution has not changed at all down the centuries, is a theoretical possibility, but has never been seriously advanced by anyone, so far as I am aware. Nevertheless, it may have been broadly true, down to the First World War, at least.

bution is surveyed every twenty-five or thirty years, but from this vantage point the patterns should be clear.

The first of these perspectives, that income and wealth have become more and more concentrated, is, of course, strongly associated with Marx and the Marxist view of capitalism. In *Capital* Marx wrote:

> As soon as this process of transformation has sufficiently decomposed the old society from top to bottom, as soon as the labourers are turned into proletarians, their means of labour into capital, as soon as the capitalist mode of production stands on its own feet, then the further socialization of labour and further transformation of the land and other means of production into socially exploited and, therefore, common means of production, as well as the further expropriation of private proprietors, takes a new form. That which is now to be expropriated is no longer the labourer working for himself, but the capitalist exploiting many labourers . . . One capitalist kills many . . . Along with the constantly diminishing number of the magnates of capital, who monopolize all advantages of this process of transformation, grows the mass of misery, oppression, slavery, degradation, exploitation: but with this too grows the revolt of the working class . . . (Selsam, Goldway, and Martel, 320–1).

Until a generation or so ago – that is, until the post-war Affluent Society emerged in Britain – a number of Marxist historians maintained in all seriousness that the standard of living and real wages of the British working class were indeed continually declining, while the wealthier classes in Britain were becoming steadily richer. Jürgen Kuczynski, a Marxist historian who in 1946 published *A Short History of Labour Conditions Under Industrial Capitalism in Great Britain and the Empire 1750–1944*, stated that

> During the first period [of British industrial capitalism], which began with the industrial revolution and ended somewhere around the middle of the last century . . . labour conditions deteriorated almost everywhere . . . During the second period [*c.* 1850–1900] certain groups of workers – the skilled and well-organized workers, the labour aristocracy – experienced an improvement of working and living conditions, while the great mass of the workers experienced a deterioration of living conditions . . . [In the third period, *c.* 1900–44] up to the 1914–18 war real wages had a tendency to decline, that the post-war increase was very small, and that there was not a single trade cycle during which real wages reached the level of the turn of the century . . . This lowering of the wage standard, of the purchasing

power of the working class, occurs not only among the great mass of the workers, but also among the so-called labour aristocracy. (Kuczynski, 99 and 104.)

The seventeenth-century British labourer must have received a truly princely remuneration by the standards of our impoverished time! Kuczynski's thesis, so far as I am aware, is not supported by any contemporary Marxist historians, who readily admit to a rise in working-class living standards from about 1850 onwards. Given the failure of capitalism's evolution to see the growth of the 'mass of misery, oppression, slavery, degradation, exploitation', as Marx predicted, but instead a slow but steady rise in working-class living standards, Marxist thinkers explained this by devising the concept of the 'labour aristocracy', the skilled, craft union-based working class whose wages and living standards approached those of the middle class. The bourgeoisie, according to this theory, could afford to create and maintain such a class by its exploitation of the Third World via imperialism; in return the 'labour aristocracy' acted as a break on any radical working-class political sentiment and generally aped the bourgeoisie.

Even if the strict Marxist view of a constant lowering of working-class living standards is untrue, the first view presented above, that wealth and income become ever more concentrated, might still be true if the wealthier classes became richer at a much greater rate than the incomes of the working class increased, and these differential rates of increase continued to the present. Something of the sort may well have occurred during the nineteenth century, as will be discussed shortly, but there is no credible statistical evidence to support the view that the concentration of wealth and income continued in this century. Indeed all the evidence suggests that the opposite has happened: that private wealth and income in Britain have become progressively more equally distributed in this century, a trend which may have begun in the middle to late nineteenth century. Much of this evidence, it should be noted, has been presented by explicit critics of the remaining maldistribution of wealth and income in Britain, usually in the context of an entreaty for a wealth tax and greater economic equality.

That the strict Marxist view of continuing and progressive inequality is not borne out by any credible historical evidence may be seen from a parenthetical discussion of the notion of 'finance capital' in the evolution of the British economy. Above we saw that in the 1860s Marx believed that the 'magnates of capital' would 'kill' many other capitalists as capitalism moved into a higher stage. Some Marxist theorists who wrote after Marx's death, like the Austrian Rudolf Hilferding, laid increasing stress on the development of 'finance capital' as a further stage in the evolution of capitalism, wherein a few super-magnates of big business, and especially the wealthy bankers, would gain ever greater control over the total economy, eliminating small and medium-sized businesses by swallowing them up. America, with its Morgans, Fords, and Rockefellers, as well as Germany and possibly some other European states, might plausibly be said to have evolved more and more in a way which Marx and Marxists predicted (ignoring such concerns as the key importance of ethnic and sectional factors in America's development), at least down to 1914 and possibly afterwards. But it is significant that this notion cannot be applied to the British experience with any real plausibility. British finance, as is well known, mainly steered clear of any large-scale investment in British industry: the City of London and the industrial towns of northern Britain largely went their own way. Although there was a growth of 'trusts' and cartels in many spheres of British business life in the late nineteenth century, this proceeded much more slowly than in Germany or America. Similarly, British millionaires were only fractionally as wealthy as the peak American multi-millionaires of the 'gilded' age of Carnegie, Vanderbilt, Astor and many others.

Many Marxists (and others) would probably explain the failure of 'finance capital' to emerge in Britain both before 1914 and afterwards by a number of factors rooted in Britain's peculiar historical evolution: the historical and long-standing separation of the City of London and the manufacturing north, divided not merely by physical distance but by such social and cultural factors as the relative strength of Anglicanism and nonconformity; the wealth and political leadership of the landed aristocracy; the 'haemorrhage of talent' as the public school educated sons of successful businessmen entered the gentry and joined the idle rich; and the key importance of the Empire and overseas trade in luring investment away from British industry. Whatever the truth or relevance of these factors, it is the case that Britain failed to produce an ever smaller but ever wealthier and more powerful business elite along the lines of strict Marxist theory.

All of the historical evidence which does exist on long-term trends in the distribution of wealth and income in Britain since the Industrial Revolution points squarely to the second or third of the broad historical viewpoints noted above as being true. Because of the lack of really adequate historical data prior to this century, especially in the area of wealth (rather than income) distribution, which of these two views is the more accurate cannot be determined with absolute accuracy, although most economic historians would probably accept the second as being the more likely to be true.

Probably the earliest economist to theorize about such long-term trends in economic inequality was Simon Kuznets, the American Nobel Prize winner. In his presidential address to the American Economic Association printed in 1955 as 'Economic Growth and Income Inequality'[6] Kuznets theorized that levels of inequality during long-term periods of modern economic growth first rose and then fell in a manner which resembled an 'inverted U'. Greater inequality was one outcome of industrialization, while greater equality is a product of the post-industrial period.

The first and best known attempt empirically to assess this matter for a very long period of British history was undertaken by Lee Soltow, an American economic historian, in 1968. Soltow's study of 'Long-Run Changes in British Income Inequality'[7] is an extremely sophisticated and economically numerate view of long-term British income distribution which ranges in time from 1436(!) to 1962–3. Soltow has employed the famous studies of income and social class presented by Gregory King for 1688, by Patrick Colquhoun for 1801–3 and 1812, by Dudley Baxter for 1867, Arthur Bowley for 1880 and 1913, and the official Inland Revenue income tax statistics for 1962–3, rearranging the data in statistical and graphical form to indicate income inequality in each period; additionally, he has included a number of further studies, including H.L. Gray's paper on 'Income from Land in England in 1436', specifically to study high income groups.

Soltow's paper contains two graphs which summarize his findings and are easy for anyone to follow. The first (Figure 1) plots vertically the percentage of *total income* of persons at a particular time with an income less than X, while, horizontally, it measures the percentage of *persons* at that time with incomes less than income

X. This kind of graph is called a Lorenz Curve after its originator, and is very useful to plot degrees of inequality.

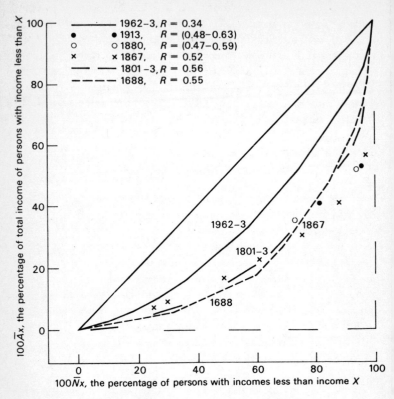

Figure 1 Lorenz Curve of British income inequality, 1688–1963

The graph is arranged by percentages, which means that total income must be divided into smaller percentile groups to indicate high, moderate and low incomes. If everyone in Britain received precisely the same income, the straight diagonal line would represent this situation. The closer the actual line of income inequality at a particular date approaches to this line, the more equal (in income terms) that society is; the further away to the right-hand side of the diagram the actual line (or dot, where there is insufficient data) is, the greater the degree of inequality. Where there is a dot or dots rather than a line, the closer to the upper right-hand corner the dot is, the greater the degree of inequality.

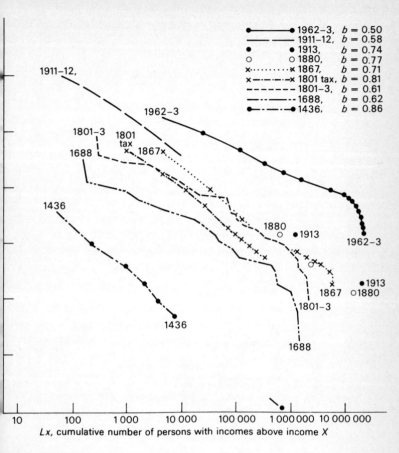

Figure 2 Cumulative frequency distributions of incomes of persons in Great Britain, 1436–1963

Soltow's second graph (Figure 2), which measures only higher income groups, employs a different type of graph (known technically as a Pareto Curve). In this graph, the vertical axis indicates income in pounds, the horizontal axis the number of persons with income in excess of an amount X as indicated on the vertical curve which is arranged logarithmically. In this graph, perfect income equality would be indicated by a flat line, and the flatter the line the more equal incomes are at a particular time.

[61]

Before turning to Soltow's conclusions, it is important to emphasize that Soltow's income figures are taken from a wide range of historical estimates. With the exception of his 1801 figures (taken from the Income Tax Returns, but nonetheless believed to

TABLE 2: King's estimates of incomes in England and Wales for 1688

No. of families in class	Class	Yearly income per family (£)
160	Temporal lords	3200
26	Spiritual lords	1300
800	Baronets	880
600	Knights	650
3000	Esquires	450
12,000	Gentlemen	280
5000	Persons in greater offices and places	240
5000	Persons in lesser offices and places	120
2000	Eminent merchants and traders by sea	400
8000	Lesser merchants and traders by sea	198
10,000	Persons in the law	154
2000	Eminent clergymen	72
8000	Lesser clergymen	50
40,000	Freeholders of the better sort	91
120,000	Freeholders of the lesser sort	55
150,000	Farmers	42½
16,000	Persons in liberal arts and sciences	60
50,000	Shopkeepers and tradesmen	45
60,000	Artisans and handicrafts	38
5000	Naval officers	80
4000	Military officers	60
35,000	Common soldiers	14
50,000	Common seamen	20
364,000	Labouring people and out-servants	15
400,000	Cottagers and paupers	6½
30,000 (persons)	Vagrants, beggars, gipsies, thieves and prostitutes	2 (per head)

be a considerable undercounting of incomes at that time) and the twentieth-century data, all of these figures are estimates which in some cases are little more than good guesses and lack any factual confirmation. For instance, in the late seventeenth century Gregory King produced his celebrated *Natural and Political Obser-*

vations Upon the State and Condition of England, which divided the English population into twenty-six 'classes', estimating the total incomes, average incomes, expenses, and so on of each group.[8] (This is included in the data in Table 2.) Living-in domestic servants and boarders were counted with each 'class' – as part of a 'family' – rather than separately. The twenty-six classes begin with 160 'Temporall Lords' and their families, 26 Spiritual Lords, 800 baronets, 600 knights, and 3000 'Esquires', down to 364,000 families of 'labouring people and outservants', 400,000 'cottagers and paupers' and 30,000 'vagrants' (individuals, not families). These classes are by turns legally defined groups (as with the knights and baronets), occupations (as with farmers and 'shopkeepers and tradesmen'), social categories, often vague in nature (as with 12,000 'gentlemen', and 16,000 'persons in sciences and liberal arts'), and miscellaneous catch-alls (as with the 60,000 'artizans and handycrafts'). Naturally, any such national estimate made in 1688 was an incredible feat, and King's overall population figures are regarded as remarkably accurate. Nevertheless, both the numbers in King's individual classes – his 10,000 'persons in the law' and 16,000 'persons in sciences and liberal arts' sound far too high, while King probably underestimated merchants, shopkeepers and labourers, and underestimated artisans and workers in industrial trades – and his income totals are obviously subject to very wide margins of error and are lacking in any official confirmation. Two recent American economic historians have argued that King underestimated total British income by 25.1 per cent (Lindert and Williamson, 'Reinterpreting', 390–4). Furthermore, the twenty-six classes in King's study each include a wide range of incomes and arriving at an average for each class seems extremely difficult. If one were asked to estimate the average income of a variegated social or occupational category – say, shopkeepers or widows living alone – and had no official data to help, even good and well informed guesses would be subject to extremely wide margins of error. To take the example of today's shopkeepers, would an average shopkeeper's income be £7500 – or £15,000 – or less – or more? Who could say, without further evidence? King no doubt had plausible enough reasons for making his class estimates, but these estimates cannot be taken uncritically.

Unfortunately, and despite the great increase in statistical and economic data of all sorts in modern times, the nineteenth-century estimates used by Soltow rest on no firmer base. Between 1801 and 1911, because of the Schedule System employed by the Inland Revenue, one cannot determine the number of individual persons with an income liable to income tax (generally, at least £150 or £160 per year). Dudley Baxter's estimates for 1867 were the most comprehensive mid-Victorian attempt to measure the distribution of individual income. Like King he was a careful and ingenious worker who had, of course, a much wider range of official sources to work with than was the case in the seventeenth century. Nevertheless, Baxter's lower income figures are not based upon any official statistics, while his statistics for the tax-paying classes are severely handicapped by the fact that the number of individual tax payers is unknown. Baxter claimed that unspecified 'official authority' had supplied him with the number of individual tax payers, but Josiah Stamp, possibly the greatest expert on this subject, wrote in 1916 that Baxter had overestimated the number of tax payers by 40 per cent. At the other end of the scale, Baxter assumed that there were no really wageless families in Britain, and Britain's paupers were a rotating group of workers occasionally in employment, occasionally unemployed.

Later historians like Harold Perkin have attempted to wrestle with these and other considerations in assessing the accuracy of Baxter; the point is that though rationally argued revisions in Baxter and other pre-twentieth century investigators of national income can be advanced, the lack of official statistics on income distribution makes these only plausible assumptions.

Statistics on income distribution in this century such as Soltow's for 1962–3 are generally derived from the income tax data by range of income as stated in *The Annual Report of the Inland Revenue*. Unlike the situation in the last century, these are official figures (although they contain an element of estimation), and are compiled by the taxation authorities of the British government. One must, therefore, assume that they are accurate, although a number of salient facts should be kept in mind: they are initially figures for gross rather than net incomes, that is, incomes before tax (although the Inland Revenue does also offer statistics on the distribution of incomes after tax); there is the unknowable factor of tax avoidance; capital gains and losses are not included in these figures, nor are incomes from two or more members of the same household aggregated; neither fringe benefits nor home production – for instance the growing of one's own foodstuffs – are included; many other similar considerations have been pointed out by economists who have analysed this question in detail. (Atkinson, *Economics*, Chapter 4.)

In view of the seemingly formidable nature of the drawbacks of the historical evidence from which Soltow's conclusions are derived, one may wonder whether they are not very much lacking in credibility. This supposition would be a mistake, although the pitfalls of the evidence must clearly be kept in mind. In all likelihood, the broad patterns which Figures 1 and 2 seem to indicate are, within a reasonable margin of error, close enough to reality to be accepted.

It will be seen from Figures 1 and 2 that there appears to be a most unfortunate and striking gap in the long-term historical income distribution figures prepared by Soltow – between 1688 and 1867, these figures include income distribution data for only one period – 1801–3 – derived from Patrick Colquhoun's two *Treatises* which included a 'class' table very similar to Gregory King's, and from the official income tax figures for 1801.[9] The entire period which saw the origins and completion of Britain's industrialization is thus almost completely lacking in cogent evidence on income distribution – and unfortunately, given the nature of the taxation and other official statistics which do exist, it is unlikely that today's economic historians will be able to reconstruct the evolution of income distribution in Britain during the period of industrialization with any precision.

Surveying the historical evidence he has amassed, Soltow comes to several conclusions in his article. Considering Figure 1, covering the whole range of incomes, he concludes that 'the tentative hypothesis is that long-run inequality did not change in the eighteenth and nineteenth centuries. Only since the First World War has there been a decrease, and this decrease has been substantial.' Taking a longer range view, one extending back to the pre-industrial era, 'It would seem that the onslaught of the Industrial Revolution, with growth in profits from trade and professional income, could not have introduced an element of greater inequality than that existing with property [i.e. landed] income – that is, the sort of income which predominates in all pre-industrial societies.' Finally, 'there was a continued widening of opportunity for non-propertied income groups. Statistical evidence indicates that income inequality, particularly in upper income groups, has decreased for several centuries. This trend has been accelerated in the twentieth century.' Soltow's conclusions thus seem to be a blend of the second and third views above and Soltow appears to believe that the Industrial Revolution was productive of a society which was from its nature more equal than any pre-industrial society based upon landownership. Nevertheless, the tentative conclusion from Figure 1 is that the first effects of the Industrial Revolution may well have been to create greater income inequality rather than less. The American economic historians Peter H. Lindert and Jeffrey G. Williamson, who have recently analysed much of the same sources as those used by Soltow, but with greater accuracy and in more detail, tentatively reach a conclusion which seems to confirm the second of the three views put above:

> 1867 looks like a watershed. Sometime around this mid-Victorian benchmark an episodic shift took place. It now appears that income inequality declined for at least a century after 1867. [Our research] also suggests that the 1860s were preceded by at least a century of rising inequality. The early rise in inequality seems to have characterized the whole income spectrum. From 1688 to 1801/03, the top 35 per cent in the income ranks gained larger shares of the pie at the expense of both the bottom 40 per cent and the middle group . . . Between 1801/3 and 1867 the widening continued, but with a different twist: the top 5 and 10 per cent gained enormously; the unskilled bottom 40 per cent gained slightly, while those in the middle got squeezed. (Lindert and Williamson, 'Revising', 33, 36.)

These historians calculate that the Gini coefficient* of inequality rose from .468 in 1688, to .487 in 1759, .519 in 1801–3, .551 in 1867 for England and Wales (and .538 for the United Kingdom), then declined to .520 in 1880 and .502 in 1913, according to their reworking of the figures of King, Colquhoun, Baxter and others. (*Ibid*, 34). The share of the national income held by the top 10 per cent of income earners rose from 42.0 per cent in 1688 to 52.4–52.7 per cent in 1867, then declined slightly to 49.8 per cent in 1913; at the same time, the share of the bottom 40 per cent declined from 15.4 per cent in 1688 to 13.4 per cent in 1801–3, and rose to

---

*The 'Gini coefficient' is a standard measurement of inequality used by economists. The nearer the figure approaches to 1.000, the greater the degree of inequality, the nearer to zero, the greater the degree of equality.

.4.8–15.2 per cent in 1867 and 17.2 per cent in 1913. (*Ibid*, 34). Although this pattern is likely to be accurate, and probably these calculations represent the limits to which, without further and fresh evidence, our exact knowledge of this subject can reach (but see below) a number of points ought not to be ignored. The first is that the earlier estimates of income distribution – by King, Massie and Colquhoun – and indeed the nineteenth-century estimates as well, probably cannot be taken literally even with the most sophisticated patching up. Secondly, despite the Colquhoun income tax figures of 1801–3, there is a massive gap in our knowledge for over a century between Massie in 1759 and Baxter in 1867, a period which coincided with Britain's industrialization and transformation from a rural to an urban nation. Surprisingly, it appears that no well-informed contemporary observer attempted quantitatively to address the question of whether industrialization and urbanization affected the distribution of Britain's incomes, and the dearth of surviving relevant quantitative evidence makes a calculation of this by later historians in our time extremely difficult. Perhaps the question may never be comprehensively answered.

Additionally, before assuming that the second of the views put above is the most accurate, it is worth asking this question: if between, say, 1750 and 1860, Britain's income distribution became more unequal one must ask – more unequal compared to what? The answer must be to a preexisting agricultural society. But was income in such a society really more equally distributed than in one which was industrializing? Soltow has again attempted to address

TABLE 3: Landownership in England, 1873

Class	No. of owners	Acres (ooos)
Peers and peeresses	400	5728
Great landowners	1288	8497
Squires	2529	4319
Greater yeomen	9585	4782
Lesser yeomen	24,412	4144
Small proprietors	217,049	3931
Cottagers	703,289	151
Public bodies	14,459	1443
Waste		1524
Total	973,011	34,519

this question by comparing the distribution of landed income found by the official Parliamentary survey, *The Return of Owners of Land* of 1874–6, with Colquhoun's 1801–3 estimates of the distribution of incomes among twenty 'emerging groups' – shop-keepers, manufacturers, merchants, etc. (Landownership may have become somewhat more unequally distributed between 1801–3 and 1874–6, but it was basically very similar.) Soltow (p. 96) concludes that this 'new element . . . has not increased total inequality . . .'

In fact, and whatever might be imagined in advance, it is difficult to see how income in an industrializing society is likely to be more unequally distributed than income in a purely agricultural society, especially in Britain with its unique 'triple division' of agriculture among landowners, farmers, and agricultural labourers. The annual income of the greatest landowners even in the eighteenth century totalled £20,000 or more, while agricultural labourers earned possibly £12 or £15 per year (plus a further 'income' in kind) and it is evident from the 1874–6 distribution of landed incomes that agricultural ownership was extremely unequal. This Victorian survey of landownership, moreover, substantially under-states the degree of inequality in agricultural society, since the annual income of nearly every landowner in Britain was consider-ably higher than that of any of the hundreds of thousands of agricultural labourers or of most farmers, whose incomes are *not* included in the Parliamentary *Return of Owners of Land*. Although Britain had no peasantry, its agricultural income divisions prior to the Industrial Revolution were possibly as great as in continental Europe, since its landed elite was immeasurably richer than most continental aristocracies.

Britain was never, of course, a purely landed society, and already before industrialization contained both an urban middle class and its rural equivalent of farmers, smaller landowners and rural trades-men. Although the effect of industrialization was to create a new middle class of industrialists and other businessmen as well as to increase the number of clerks and 'white collar' office staff, surpris-ingly little actual evidence exists which points to a sharp and sudden increase in the number and wealth of business magnates, especially before the mid-nineteenth century, or even to a phen-omenal growth in the income of the middle classes at this time. From 1803–4 to 1814–15, for instance, the total value of individual incomes assessed under Schedule D – the tax on businesses and the professions – to income tax (i.e. incomes of £60 or more) rose only from £34.9 million to £37.1 million, while the total of incomes assessed under Schedule A of the income tax – the tax on rents from lands – rose from £38.7 million to £60.1 million. Even in 1850 the totals assessed under Schedules A and D were, respectively, £91.7 million and £64.9 million.[10] Similarly – though this is a measure of wealth, not of income – personal estates of £100,000 left at death rose from an annual average of 16.5 per year in 1809–14 to 29.0 per year in 1825–9. Thereafter, rather surprisingly, they hardly rose at all until around 1860. The average number left in the years 1845–9 was only 29.2. Although the middle classes obviously grew in size and importance, this was in the context of a nation with a large, pre-existing middle class dating from long before industrialization, and some historians have seriously questioned whether middle-class opportunities, especially in the professions, widened enormously in the nineteenth century.

Additionally, some fresh evidence can be offered here about the likely course of income distribution in Britain during the nineteenth century. Although no statistics survive from the income tax about the range of individual incomes, it is nevertheless possible to ascertain with a fair degree of accuracy the relative proportion of

TABLE 4: Percentage of British incomes earned by tax payers and non-tax payers

| | Income tax payers, by category | | | | | | |
	Landed	% of British income	Business and professionals	% of British income	British gross national income	Non-tax payers' income	%
1810:							
£60+	110.3	36.6	49.3	16.4	301.1	141.5	50.0
£150+	90.4	30.0	36.4	12.1	301.1	174.3	57.9
1850–1	128.3	24.5	106.0	20.3	523.3	289.0	55.2
1860–1	145.1	21.7	152.9	22.9	668.0	370.0	55.4
1870–1	188.7	20.6	209.8	22.9	916.6	518.1	56.5
1880–1	225.6	21.5	301.2	28.7	1051.2	524.4	49.9
1890–1	232.3	18.0	410.9	31.9	1288.2	645.0	50.1
1900–1	265.6	16.2	555.4	33.8	1642.9	821.9	50.0

national income going to persons with incomes below £150* (£60 during the first income tax), the great majority of whom were working-class men and women. Although this exercise requires many reworkings of published income tax data, it is a relatively simple procedure, and that no one has apparently attempted it before is somewhat curious.

Table 4 presents these results. Because of the vagaries of the income tax figures, they are certainly not accurate to within more than a few per cent, but the broad trends are clear enough. The gross income assessed from among all tax payers has been further divided into 'landed' and 'business/professional' portions, based upon the Schedules of the income tax.[11] It should also be noted that the minimum level of liability for the Schedule D of the income tax has been taken as £150 throughout the period covered (from Stamp's figures[12]) while Ireland has been excluded from these figures wherever possible. The gross national income figures, used here, taken from estimates by Deane and Cole, are estimates which other historians may dispute.

Bearing in mind the margin of error concealed in the figures in Table 4, several points appear clear. As one would expect, there is a continuing and clear-cut shift, among taxable income, from land to the businesses and professions in the nineteenth century, although this trend by no means proceeds as rapidly as some might imagine, and landed income (in part because urban rents are included) is still a very significant factor in the British national income in 1900. Concerning the distribution of income, there is remarkably little evidence of any increase in inequality until the 1870s, when the percentage of national income going to the poorer classes sharply *decreases* after remaining almost steady since 1810. This is especially surprising since this occurred at almost precisely the date when income equalization trends should have first begun, according to most historians. One factor clearly at work here is the fact that there probably was a gradual increase in the pay of the lower middle and skilled working classes in the late nineteenth century, with many more lower white collar and even skilled manual workers now exceeding £150 in income than previously, together with an ever increasing number of tax payers. Along with this,

---

*The lower limit of liability for income tax was £100 from 1853 to 1876. The data in Table 4 takes £150 as the lower limit of liability throughout.

however, may well have occurred a marked increase, beginning around 1870, in very high business incomes (and fortunes), for which there is evidence from the probate records. It is possible that the estimates of income inequality taken by Soltow for this period have not sufficiently taken the *fin-de-siècle* growth of plutocratic incomes into account. The main point to emerge from Table 4, however, is that there is little evidence for a marked diminution in the proportion of small incomes among all British incomes during the period of industrialization and Britain's industrial zenith. It is possible that such a diminution occurred before 1810, but no comparable statistics exist, and the earlier such a process began, the less plausible it becomes to see this as an outcome of the Industrial Revolution. In 1810 Britain's Industrial Revolution was far from complete, and many historians, indeed, would question its decisive impact prior to the railway age of the 1830s and 1840s. The evidence in Table 4, if taken at face value, points to the poor majority as almost precisely maintaining an equal slice of the British national income cake throughout the first three-quarters of the nineteenth century, but the evidence contains a fairly wide element of error, and is too chronologically limited before 1850 to be decisive.

One primary and essential fact of demographic history is, however, undeniable, namely that Great Britain's total population grew enormously, from perhaps 7.5 million in 1750 to nearly 12 million in 1811 to 23.1 million in 1861. Such a rate of sustained growth was without precedent in human history. In my view, a proper consideration of this factor basically alters the context of any historical investigation of British income distribution. Britain's population grew by over 200 per cent in just over a century, and Britain contained nearly 16 million more mouths to feed in 1861 than in 1750. It would be remarkable if any society which grew in numbers at this unprecedented rate could maintain an undiminished standard of living, and if Britain's income distribution became more uneven, this is really less surprising than that the unevenness of its distribution altered as little as it seems to have done between 1695 or 1750 and 1867. The reason for this is that unprecedented population growth was accompanied by equally unprecedented economic growth, in which the working classes evidently shared, however unevenly, at least much of the time. Although the incomes of the wealthier classes were growing in the period of industrialization, those of the working classes were growing as well, and, if less rapidly, mainly because their numbers were increasing more quickly still. Additionally, it should not be forgotten that the investment necessary for Britain's industrialization – the money to build its factories, canals, railways, and docks – had to come almost entirely from private sources, and that much of the income (as it were) 'sacrificed' by entrepreneurs and workers alike went into economic expansion. This has been the case in all societies undergoing industrialization, and totalitarian societies which rapidly industrialized, like Stalin's Russia, have often made the deliberate sacrifice of current consumer goods and living standards in the interests of capital investment, especially in the heavy industries, a primary state goal. Those fortunate societies, like the nineteenth-century United States, which could simultaneously enjoy massive investment, economic growth, and clearly rising living standards, enjoyed such advantages as a result of abundant free land on the frontier, a relative labour shortage, and ample foreign investment. These advantages Britain of the Industrial Revolution period certainly did not enjoy, and if Britain did manage to experience a fairly limited diminution in living standards (and possibly none at all) while undergoing the world's first Industrial Revolution and unprecedented population growth, this should surely be counted as a considerable credit to British society. The evidence on income distribution remains unsatisfactory, but it points as well to, at most, a limited rearrangement of incomes in favour of the rich in the context of a working class which had increased immeasurably in size.

Income distribution during the inter-war period

The date at which this trend to increasing income inequality began to be reversed – when income distribution began unequivocally to become more equal – is also a matter of dispute. Most economic historians point to the inter-war period as something of a watershed, although the data available to the historian is far from perfect. Very broadly, the overall situation of income distribution in Britain between 1918 and 1939 seemed to be marked by the following main features.

(a) The general economic and social structure of British society was much as before the First World War; that is, there was a very considerable degree of income and wealth inequality within the capitalist system.

(b) Nevertheless, there was clearly an increase in the economic wellbeing of the working classes. Real money wages (i.e. the type of weekly income earned by the majority of the working classes) increased much faster than salaries (i.e. the type of earnings, often paid fortnightly or monthly, earned by the white collar middle classes) and there was a considerable diminution of primary poverty.

(c) At the other end of the scale, there was probably some diminution in very large pre-tax incomes, especially those based on agricultural rentals, income from abroad, or from old staple industries (cotton, engineering, shipbuilding, coalmining) heavily affected by the post-1918 economic decline.

(d) This diminution in very large incomes was greatly affected by a marked rise in rates of income taxes, which now had an appreciable effect upon high income earners; conversely, government transfer payments to the poor became a significant element in overall welfare for the first time.

(e) This broad picture is also affected by a number of factors either original to the post-1918 period or *sui generis* to it, especially very high levels of unemployment, considerable regional differences in wages (mainly reflecting the decline of the staple industries of northern and Celtic Britain), a substantial growth in the number of relatively lower paid women workers, and a decline in the average family size. These factors pull in several ways, but they tended to disadvantage still further those workers most heavily affected by the decline of the old staple industries after 1918 and to advantage further those workers and the salaried middle classes based in the service or newer industries and situated mainly in the south of England.

The problem of ascertaining the course of income distribution during the inter-war period is compounded by the continuing inadequacy of income statistics. From 1909 onwards, the so-called 'super tax' (known as the 'surtax' from 1929) was levied on incomes over £5000, a figure that was progressively lowered by steps to £2000 in 1920. For that reason, for the first time we have good statistics on very high incomes. Additionally, there are the continuing statistics of the ordinary income tax although its minimum liability was also altered from £150 to £500. But because income tax was not levied on low, typically working-class incomes, there are still no official and comprehensive statistics for working-class incomes or for the entire population.

The inter-war period did, however, see the beginning of the *concerted* use of *modern* techniques of survey research, that is, widespread studies of a particular town derived from interviews with a random sample or a complete sample of households; the data derived from information provided verbally by each householder and aimed at ascertaining household incomes and living standards, especially of the working classes. These were, of course, not an entirely new development. Charles Booth's classic and monumental survey of living standards in London appeared in 1889, while Joseph Rowntree's important study of poverty in York was published a decade later. The inter-war period saw the appearance of similar studies in twelve cities and towns as well as a national survey of food consumption and total expenditure in 1938. These surveys concentrated on the working classes – we know rather less about the dimensions of middle-class incomes in this period – while rural England and the Celtic areas were less well surveyed; as was suburbia. Yet they provide realistic and revealing data on living standards which are extremely suggestive about the overall distribution of income and the extent of poverty in Britain.

These surveys, together with whatever exists in the way of official statistics on pay and wages, suggest that real but not decisive gains were made by the working classes during the inter-war period, although unemployment also reached record levels at this time. Average annual money wage earnings – that is, the weekly pay received by most of the working class – increased by 103.0 per cent between 1911–13 and 1938, while average annual salary earnings – that is, white collar and managerial earnings – increased by only 17.4 per cent (Aldcroft, 357). Most of these gains came in the immediate post-war period, with both wages and salaries rising sharply from 1918 to 1924 and then stagnating until the outbreak of the next war.

According to all of the evidence, there was a decline in primary poverty during the inter-war period and a rise in working-class real incomes, despite the Depression. Arthur L. Bowley addressed the question *Has Poverty Diminished?* in his book of 1924. Even since 1913, he found, the proportion of families in poverty had fallen to just over half, while if unemployment had not risen but remained at its pre-war levels, this proportion would have declined by two-thirds. In York, Rowntree found that only 44 per cent of the proportion of families living in poverty in 1899 were still in poverty in 1936. The average income of working-class families in Bristol in 1937 was twice the minimum level regarded by researchers as indicating poverty. Nevertheless, primary poverty of the old kind still existed – 10.3 per cent of all families in Bristol in 1937 were living in absolute poverty, while a further 19.3 per cent enjoyed what this study considered an 'insufficient income' for even a minimal level of decency. Bristol was relatively prosperous, and the percentage of such families in the depressed areas of northern Britain must have been far higher (Aldcroft, 386).

The 'normal' working-class income was now, for possibly the first time in British history, above the subsistence level, and increasing portions of working-class budgets were spent on non-necessities and even household durable items like radios. There were nearly 9 million radio licences by 1940, meaning that the great majority of even working-class households must have owned a radio by the outbreak of the war. Persistent patterns of poverty were related to high rates of unemployment – although a minimal system of relief was now in force – to the number of children in a family, to old age, and to such fortuitous factors as the health of the breadwinner. Except for the admittedly all-important factor of high unemployment, poverty had thus become recognizably modern in its instances and akin to the situation in the post-1945 Welfare State; it no longer automatically accompanied working-class life as it had for much of the nineteenth century. The economic historian Sidney Pollard noted the changes in working-class life in these decades:

> Statistics fail to take full account of the differences made by electricity instead of candles, and gas cookers instead of coal or coke ranges, as standard equipment in working-class homes; of improved housing, including indoor water and sanitation; or of radio, the cinema and newspapers within almost everyone's reach.
> (Cited in John Stevenson, 129).

Qualitatively as well as quantitatively, the picture had also improved considerably since before 1914–18. Although the middle classes increased in relative size in the inter-war period, this increase was uneven in nature. The number and income of self-employed persons declined at the time, the percentage of occupied persons who were self-employed dropping from 14 per cent in 1911 to 6 per cent by 1931. To balance this there was a very substantial increase in the number of salary earners in Britain, from 8.3 per cent of the occupied population in 1911 to 14.3 per cent in 1938. Overall, the percentage of middle-class persons in the whole population probably rose slightly because of the increase in white collar jobs, but this growth was unspectacular in nature, and the reason many more people seemed to be living in a middle-class manner than before the war was probably because of increased affluence of the working classes, together with cultural and social changes like the spread of media-influenced 'classless values', clothing, and the like. Nearly all of this increase would have come in London and the south of England.[13]

It is also likely that the First World War had a major impact upon the incomes of the rich. This was due not so much to any decline in the number of high income earners, whose number actually increased between the Edwardian period and the 1920s, as to the combined effects of inflation and taxation. The cost of living nearly doubled in Britain between 1913 and 1923; although it declined somewhat during the Depression, it was still markedly higher than before the war. Meanwhile, marginal rates of income tax and the 'super tax' – the special income tax on very high income – rose very considerably, even in peacetime. By the 1920s, the affluent classes came to accept as normal rates of taxation which they would have unhesitatingly described as 'communistic' only a decade before and which the most extreme radical politician would have hesitated before proposing. In 1913, a bachelor earning £10,000 a year – an enormous sum – retained £9242 after paying income tax and super tax; by 1922 – that is, after Conservative-dominated governments had held office for seven years – he would have retained only £5672, and, despite some further tax relief, he would have retained between £5672 and £6968 after each budget during the inter-war period (Butler and Sloman, 137–8). Many socialists would point out that this man still retained more than enough; but the point is that no one, before 1914, could possibly imagine that Tory governments would take so much, especially in pounds worth only half of their previous value. The growing willingness of wealthier persons to accept much higher rates of taxation as normal is sometimes termed the 'displacement effect' by economists.

The combined effect of taxation and inflation upon Britain's top income earners was almost certainly very considerable. According to A.L. Bowley:

> The effect of this on the number of the rich, say those with £10,000 or more [in 1914 and 1924–5] was very marked. Before taxation there were nearly 5000 such incomes in 1914, and 9200 in 1925; but if we count income after taxation only 4000 reached £10,000 in 1914 and about 4120 in 1925.
>
> But to get an equivalent to the £10,000 of 1914, about £18,000 is needed in 1925 to meet the rise in prices; and to leave £18,000 net it is necessary to have more than £30,000 gross, and only 1300 incomes reached this amount. Hence the number of the rich, defined as those who had £10,000 to spend (or save) in 1914 and the equivalent amount in 1925, had fallen from 4000 to 1300 (Bowley, 137–8).

The effect of income taxation alone was to reduce the share of the top 1 per cent of all income recipients from 29 to 24.4 per cent in 1938, while raising the share of lower income groups from 55.5 to 59.6 per cent (Aldcroft, 389, citing Seers). This does not seem on the face of it like a cataclysmic change but it conceals the further effects of inflation and the increasing use of public money for welfare expenditure, patchy as that was before 1945. Bowley concludes:

> The general result of the whole system of taxation, wage adjustments, and social expenditure has been a very marked redistribution of the National Income . . . The very rich have less than half their pre-war income (allowing for taxes and changes of prices); the least well off of the working class have gained most (Bowley, 160).

Aldcroft refers to this process as one of 'levelling up', and notes that the trend in this period was 'towards a greater equality of incomes', in the context of a 'still very uneven' overall distribution of income (Aldcroft, 388, 390). This is probably the best judgement on the state of affairs which the First World War had produced.

Such a judgement is thus consistent with the second view of long-term rates of inequality advanced at the beginning of this chapter. Much of the gains for equality between 1914 and 1939 were caused by the increasing complexity and diversity of society, broadly considered, and especially the growth of a white collar salaried class. The relative increase in most working-class wages was caused by a variety of factors, including severe labour shortages during the

1914–18 war, increased trade union power, and the growth of new industries. Real family incomes were affected advantageously by a general decline in family size, with fewer children to feed and raise on average than in previous generations. For those workers who continued to hold employment, these gains were not negated by the Depression.

Income distribution in the post-war world

It seems likely in retrospect that the inter-war period marked a turning point in modern British income distribution, with a definite, though probably small, redistribution trend unequivocally beginning at this time (although its origins probably occurred earlier). Whatever qualms the historian may have with a clear-cut verdict on income redistribution between 1914 and 1939, there seems no doubt at all that the period since the outbreak of the Second World War has seen a fairly steady levelling of income distribution compared with the inter-war era.

Possibly the single most important chronological and causal locus of this clear-cut trend to income equality was the Second World War and the immediate post-war period of socialism and Austerity. Indeed, many critics and observers of British society, especially on the left, have argued that this was the *only* significant period of income redistribution in modern times, and the period since the late 1940s has seen an end to further redistributionist tendencies. This point of view was given its classic presentation in Richard M. Titmuss' well-known and searching study of *Income Distribution and Social Change* (1962). Titmuss (198) noted that

> . . . there is more than a hint from a number of studies that income inequality has been increasing since 1949 whilst the ownership of wealth . . . has probably become still more unequal . . .

Whatever the accuracy of such a contention (which will be examined below), there is general agreement that the Second World War and immediate post-war period saw what the Royal Commission on the Distribution of Income and Wealth (which reported in 1979) described as 'a significant change in the distribution [of income]' between 1938 and 1949 (cited in Atkinson (1980), 77). In 1938, according to official government statistics, the top 1 per cent of all income earners possessed 16.6 per cent of the pre-tax national income and 12.1 per cent of the post-tax national income; in 1949 these figures were, respectively, 11.2 and 6.4 per cent. These two figures for the top 10 per cent of all tax payers were (for 1938) 38.8 and 34.4 per cent and (for 1949) 33.2 and 27.1 per cent. Another economist who has examined income distribution in post-war Britain in detail, Thomas Stark, stated that 'I think we can safely conclude that the degree of inequality . . . was much less in 1963 than 1937', and it is clear that the period between 1937 and 1949 surveyed in his research witnessed a considerable increase in equalitarian trends (Stark, 110–11). Most other authorities are agreed on this matter.

Plainly the main vehicles of this trend during the 1940s were the combination of record levels of taxation, especially at the highest levels, and considerable inflation, together with the institution of a full-blown Welfare State in the context of full employment and increased trade union power. Even more than in the First World War, during the Second World War the wealthy were willing to sacrifice their assets to the vital national interest, and patriotism played as great a role as anything else in the revolution which overtook the wealthy in this period. This period also witnessed the end of servant keeping and of much of whatever old-style display and conspicuous consumption had survived into the 1930s. The bachelor who earned £10,000 retained £6103 of this sum in 1938, but only £3138 in 1945 and £3587 in 1949, sums which had declined in real value by half during the decade.

The end of Austerity and the replacement of Labour by the Tories in 1951 saw some, but certainly not all, of these legal and fiscal pressures toward income equality lifted, and it might be expected that some reversion in income distribution toward greater inequality might be apparent from the available statistics. In fact, the data which is available shows nothing of the sort, only a steady continuation, perhaps at a slower pace, of the general trend toward income equality.

Some of these basic trends are set out in Table 5, taken from the Royal Commission on the Distribution of Income and Wealth (and commonly known as the Diamond Commission from the name of its chairman Lord Diamond, a former Labour minister, not from its subject matter) which was appointed by the Wilson Government in 1974 and reported several years later. The data for this table comes from the National Income Blue Books published by the Central Statistical Office, or Royal Commission estimates, and were supplemented by the Diamond Commission with further information on certain types of income excluded from these compilations (which are based upon income tax records). Only a rough comparison is possible with pre-war figures, which are not based upon identical statistics.

TABLE 5: Distribution of personal income in Britain, 1949 to 1976–7, by given quartile groups, before and after tax

| | Before tax | | | | | |
	1949	1954	1964	1970–1	1974–5	1976–7
Quartile Groups						
Top 1%	11.2	9.3	8.2	6.6	6.2	5.4
0–10%	33.2	30.1	29.1	27.5	26.6	25.8
11–20%	14.1	15.1	15.5	15.9	15.8	16.1
21–30%	11.1	12.4	12.6	13.2	13.1	13.3
31–40%	9.6	10.5	10.9	10.9	11.0	11.1
41–50%	8.2	8.9	9.2	9.0	9.3	9.2
51–60%		7.4	7.4	7.4	7.6	7.5
61–70%		5.3	5.8	5.9	5.8	6.0
71–80%	27.3		4.3	4.6	4.6	4.7
81–90%		10.3	5.2	3.1	3.6	3.8
91–100%			2.5	2.6	2.5

| | After taxes | | | | | |
	1949	1954	1964	1970–1	1974–5	1976–7
Top 1%	6.4	5.3	5.3	4.5	4.0	3.5
0–10%	27.1	25.3	25.9	23.9	23.2	22.4
11–20%	14.5	15.7	16.1	15.9	15.8	15.9
21–30%	11.9	13.3	12.9	13.3	13.2	13.4
31–40%	10.5	10.3	11.1	11.2	11.4	11.3
41–50%	9.5	9.1	8.8	9.5	9.4	9.4
51–60%		8.3	8.0	7.8	7.8	7.9
61–70%		6.4	5.6	6.5	6.4	6.8
71–80%	26.5		5.1	5.2	5.3	5.2
81–90%		11.6	6.5	6.6	4.4	4.6
91–100%					3.1	3.1

Table 5 presents the distribution of incomes both before and after income tax for the top one per cent of all income earners and for each ten per cent quartile group, from the highest to the lowest income earners. If all incomes were divided absolutely equally, each quartile group would account for ten per cent of all incomes, and the extent to which each sum is higher or lower than ten per cent indicates inequality.

It will be seen that there has been a continuing and fairly impressive decline in the pre-tax income of the top 1 per cent of all earners, with other high quartile groups experiencing similar declines. The position of the lower quartiles has hardly changed at all while the gains toward equality among the post-tax quartiles has been far less marked than among pre-tax groups. Apart from continuing low earnings among the very poorest groups, the persistence of such small shares of all income among the lowest quartiles is probably due to part-time and junior working. On the face of it, even in 1976–7 the lowest quartile earned only one-quarter to one-third of the median pre-tax income. The median pre-tax income in 1976–7 was £2615, and it is hardly credible that there could be any full-time workers at the time who earned only one-third of this sum (or less) – that is, about £872 *per year* – as a full-time income, a figure which was below the minimum wage. Many of these employees in the lowest quartiles were probably wives working part time, teenagers living at home, semi-retired persons, and the like; indeed, the median figure of £2615 seems questionably low, and it is very probable that if household income of family units rather than individual income were measured the tables would show considerably more equality.

Although poverty still obviously exists in the post-war world, the Welfare State and its various benefits is supposed to cushion the entire population from destitution. This it probably does, especially among elderly or handicapped persons who are unable to work. What seems to have most affected and alleviated the type of poverty which existed in the pre-war world was a mixture of much higher minimum wages for all and full employment for most manual workers – full not merely in the sense of (until 1970) very little working-class unemployment, but continuous employment throughout the active lifetime of most workers. Manual work in the post-war period is rarely if ever highly seasonal in nature, nor does it require the kind of near-vagrant tramping so common to working-class employment before 1914 or even 1939. To these factors must be added the dramatic decline in family size and in very large families and, finally, the effects of the Welfare State.[14]

The number of persons living in poverty in post-war Britain is difficult to estimate, but in the mid-1960s, when unemployment was at its lowest point, two government estimates suggested that about 5.8 per cent of the population had income below the Supplementary Benefit level (Atkinson in Wedderburn, 59). Poverty in the post-war period (prior to the upsurge in unemployment in the 1970s) was chiefly confined to the elderly, single parent families, especially those headed by women with few skills, and to special cases like the handicapped. The vast increase in unemployment during the 1970s has probably added scores of thousands of skilled workers to this group, especially in the depressed areas, while the proportion of low income blacks in the population has also probably increased. In view of this – and unemployment was already very extensive in 1976–7 – it is surprising that the position of bottom quartiles has not deteriorated further.

Turning back to Table 5, it will be seen that, although the share of the total income earned by the wealthiest *post*-tax quartile groups is much smaller than the share of these groups *before* taxes, the decline in this share between 1949 and 1976–7 has been far less pronounced. This is almost certainly the result of the fact that enormously high rates of income tax and surtax on high incomes already existed in 1949 and have been considerably eased since then. In 1949, a bachelor earning £10,000 retained only £3587 but by 1974 – when £10,000 was no more than a moderately high income rather than an enormous one – he retained £6088. In 1978, a bachelor with no dependents earning £50,000 retained £15,124, only a slightly lower percentage than the £10,000 bachelor in 1949. Indeed, the continuation of this levelling trend at the highest income levels is an interesting indication of the general trend to income levelling. In 1976–7, the after-tax income of the very wealthiest 1 per cent of the total population totalled only 3.5 per cent of all incomes; in other words, their incomes exceeded the median after-tax income by only three and a half times. This is certainly not an excessive differential, and must indicate that the number of enormous after-tax incomes is very small, at least if this data can be taken at face value.

Certainly so far as the higher income groups are concerned, and probably for the whole population, all of this data indicates a continuation of the general trend toward income redistribution in the post-war world; through the late 1970s there was, perhaps surprisingly, no good evidence at all to indicate a reversal of the trend to greater income equality since the 1950s, as some commentators have argued. This may suggest that the trend to income equality is, broadly, inherent in the contemporary British economic and social structure, and was not a function of the special conditions of the Second World War and Austerity period.

There is, however, some indication that the distribution of incomes has become slightly more unequal since 1976–7. The Central Statistical Office conducts a biannual Family Expenditure Survey based on household income – arguably a much better test of income distribution than the statistics of individual tax payers – both before and after taxes. The entire United Kingdom population is divided into fifths (and not into tenths as in Table 5), according to their 'original income' – their gross income – and their 'final income' – their net income after subtracting not merely income tax, but national insurance and adding (where relevant) all social benefits, pensions, and supplementary benefits.

TABLE 6: Distribution of original and final household income, by percentage of total income, 1976–80[15]

Original Income	Bottom Fifth	Next Fifth	Middle Fifth	Next Fifth	Top Fifth	Total
1976	0.8	9.4	18.8	26.6	44.4	100.0
1978	0.6	9.2	18.7	26.7	44.8	100.0
1980	0.5	8.5	18.6	26.9	45.5	100.0

Final Income	Bottom Fifth	Next Fifth	Middle Fifth	Next Fifth	Top Fifth	Total
1976	7.6	12.8	18.1	24.0	37.5	100.0
1978	7.2	12.5	17.9	24.0	38.4	100.0
1980	6.8	12.3	18.0	24.1	38.8	100.0

It will be seen that there has by this measurement been a small but perceptible increase in household income inequality during this period. The Central Statistical Office attributes this to 'a rise in the number of pensioner households and to increased inequality within groups of similar households' and notes that 'taxes and benefits did not counteract this increase in the spread of original income'.[16] With on one side the steady ageing of the British population and a seemingly irrevocable rise in unemployment, accompanied by rapid gains in the incomes of most white collar and skilled manual workers, it is perhaps surprising that this reversal of the trend to income equality has not proceeded faster. Along with this has gone a relative retreat, for both financial and ideological reasons, in the wide-ranging redistributionist concept of the Welfare State, a retreat (or redefinition) which one may expect to continue during the 1980s. Some limited information on the post-1980 period suggests that there has been a further slight but perceptible growth in income inequality as a result of the tax recession of the time.

Underlying what may or may not be a short-run trend, however, is a continuing long-run trend to the much greater degree of ownership of consumer durables by all households. For instance, some 59 per cent of all British households owned an automobile in 1981, a proportion up by 5 per cent since 1973, despite economic uncertainty and the ageing of the population. Ownership of refrigerators increased from 78 per cent of all households to 93 per cent in the same period, while televisions were found in 95 per cent (only!) of all households in 1973, but in 97 per cent of all households in 1981, of which 74 per cent owned a colour set.

Statistics on this subject have been collected by the General Household Survey of the Central Statistical Office, and are well worth examining for a number of reasons. First, they demonstrate clearly the possibility of continuing gains for all households in a period of rapidly rising unemployment and inflation; apparently at least a component of the long-term trend to greater and greater affluence has, paradoxically, been immune to recession. Secondly, ownership of these consumer goods is important not merely for their economic significance but for the light they shed on cultural and social values and life styles, and in particular for the transformation of the old-fashioned and traditional working-class home, with its absence of labour-saving devices, into households differing little from their middle-class counterparts. Thirdly, and related to this, is the evolution towards equality concealed in these statistics. In the nineteenth century the domestic lifes of a wealthy man in a country house and a manual worker (such as a cotton spinner) were as different as any two things could be: the rich man had a dozen servants to carry out his every domestic whim, the labourer had none, and so on *ad infinitum*. But (for example) the domestic lifes of the 93 per cent of the population with refrigerators or the 94 per cent with vacuum cleaners in 1981 were probably not dissimilar, regardless of their incomes.

TABLE 7: Possession of consumer durable goods, by household types[17]
(Percentage of all households in Great Britain with each item)

	All Households			Elderly Households*			Other Households with Children		
	1973	1978	1981	1973	1978	1981	1973	1978	1981
Vacuum Cleaner	88	92	94	83	90	92	90	94	96
Refrigerator	78	91	93	63	84	89	86	96	96
Deepfreezer	–	32	49	–	17	28	–	43	62
Washing Machine	67	75	78	48	58	61	84	90	91
Tumble Drier	–	19	23	–	9	10	–	28	37
Dishwasher	–	3	4	–	2	2	–	4	5
Telephone	45	–	75	35	–	66	50	–	79
Car	54	57	59	25	30	32	69	70	72
Central Heating	39	45	59	30	35	50	49	56	66
Television – Colour		61	74		46	61		71	83
	95			90			98		
B & W		35	23		48	35		28	17

*Defined as containing one adult aged 60 or over, or two adults, one or both aged 60 or over.

This table clearly indicates, too, that elderly households were less likely to possess any of these consumer durables than were the totality of households. The two major reasons for this are the smaller average incomes of such households, and the fact that the social mores and notions of desirable household arrangements among elderly persons were formed decades before, and elderly persons with sufficient income might not choose to possess modern appliances unknown in their youth. Nevertheless, the increase in the possession of such consumer durables as refrigerators and telephones among elderly persons has been at least as dramatic as among the entire population. The difference in economic circumstances and social habits between the elderly and the entire population is probably especially important for the discussion of wealth holding below.

Another very significant indicator of generally increasing prosperity, despite the economic setbacks of the recent past, may be pointed to from the same source. One is the extremely important matter of home ownership. Households which owned their own home (including those in the process of repaying a mortgage) rose steadily from 40 per cent of Britain's 16.2 million households in 1961 to 48 per cent of 18.2 million households in 1971 to 56 per cent of 19.5 million households in 1981.[18] Privately rented houses declined sharply between 1961 and 1981 from 34 to only 13 per cent of the total, while homes rented from a local authority or a new town rose (mainly in the 1960s) from 25 to 31 per cent in this period. A much higher percentage of households headed by professionals, employers, and managers – 62 per cent – were in the process of buying their homes with the aid of a mortgage than households with unskilled manual heads – only 16 per cent – but there must have been a very substantial increase in the percentage of skilled manual and lower white collar workers who are purchasing or have purchased their homes over the past few decades. Among households headed by 'skilled manual and own account [*sic*] nonprofessional' workers, 58 per cent either owned their homes outright (16 per cent of the total) or were purchasing them via a mortgage (42 per cent) in 1981. Even among households headed by semi-skilled manual and personal service workers, 41 per cent owned or were purchasing their homes. Apart from indicating a continuing increase in general prosperity, this pattern, it is often suggested, has wide political ramifications, with the long-term electoral decline of the Labour Party since the mid-1960s probably related to the increasing level of property ownership.

These recent trends in home ownership are a continuation of patterns which have existed during the century. To a surprising extent, however, the decisive and widespread gains for owner-occupation at the expense of other forms of tenure are the product of the recent past. It should perhaps be better realized than it is that the classical period of 'Butskellism' and the 'end of ideology' between about 1950 and 1965 occurred before the *majority* of households owned or were purchasing their own homes, although the rise in owner-occupation during this period was very marked. Taken together with Table 7, possibly no set of statistics in this book better illustrates the social and economic revolution of the twentieth century, or the shift away from privilege toward general affluence which has occurred and, evidently, is still occurring. More will be said of this important matter below.

TABLE 8: Housing by tenure, Great Britain, 1914–81, by percentage of all households[19]

Date	% Owner-Occupied	% Local Authority	% Rented from Private Landlord	% Other	Total
1914	10*	**	90		100
1938	25	10	65		100
1945	26	12	54	8	100
1951	29	18	45	8	100
1956	34	23	36	7	100
1960	42	26	26	6	100
1965	47	28	20	5	100
1970	50	30	15	5	100
1981	56	32	12	–	100

*Approximate figure; the actual range was probably between 8% and 15%.
**Included under private landlord.

Income distribution in British history: unresolved questions

Probably three main unresolved questions hang over the broad interpretation of the evidence on British income distribution. The first is whether income distribution became more unequal during the period of industrialization. The second is when a trend toward greater income equality first became established in an unequivocal way. The third is whether the clear post-1945 tendency to continuing relative income equalization is likely to be reversed because of the much higher, seemingly permanent rates of unemployment and the continuing ageing of the population in contemporary Britain.

Concerning the first of these points, it is probable that income distribution did become more unequal during the period of industrialization, although clear-cut and definitive statistical evidence on this point is lacking. Nevertheless, the fullest contemporary studies of this subject as re-examined by modern historians in the light of the best historical evidence point to some growing inequality in income between about 1760 and 1870. Two important matters must be kept in mind even if this conclusion is accepted – the vast and unprecedented growth in the British population, and the unequal distribution of pre-industrial landed wealth, indicative of a society which could hardly have been less unequal than that which succeeded it.

There may be a general belief among historians that the trend toward inequality brought about by industrialization peaked around 1867 and that thereafter this trend was reversed. There is, however, little evidence that this reversal was anything more than tentative and of limited significance until the First World War. The effects of the First World War, especially the much higher rates of taxation and inflation it brought in its wake, increased trade union membership and power, and structural changes in the economy, and were to produce a clear but not decisive trend to great income equality, especially in the period 1914–24. The Second World War accelerated this process, which continued, according to all the evidence, through the late 1970s.

Evidence from the very recent past suggests that this long-term and unequivocal trend toward greater income equality since the Second World War may now have stopped and indeed, have begun marginally to reverse, as a result of levels of unemployment unprecedented since the Depression, the ageing of the population, relative reductions in social benefits, and relatively disproportionate gains in the incomes received by the more highly paid. It is too early to know if this trend is anything more than temporary; indeed, the trend itself is as yet only a limited one. Significantly, there is no evidence at all from the ownership of consumer durables or household tenure for any recent slowing down in the long-term trend to affluence, despite the recent recession.

Returning to the three views of the long-term course of income distribution outlined at the beginning of this chapter, all of the credible evidence points to either the second or third of these propositions as having been true for the British experience: either income became more unequally distributed during the period of industrialization and has since become more equally distributed, or, very broadly, there has been no diminution of a very general trend toward ever-increasing income equality during the past two or three centuries (and probably longer). On balance, the second of the three views appears the most likely, although the data for the period of industrialization from which such a conclusion must be derived is not fully satisfactory or complete, and there may be some reasons for supposing that there was no marked increase in inequality during even this period. For the first of the three views, that income distribution has become more and more unequal, there is no evidence at all, and all of the historical evidence without exception argues directly against it.

The distribution of wealth in modern Britain

Although many crucial gaps remain in our knowledge of the evolution of income distribution in Britain since before the Industrial Revolution, perhaps even less from a long-term historical perspective is known about the course of wealth distribution in modern Britain. Some of the problems relating to ascertaining the distribution of personal wealth were discussed above. There are no estimates of wealth distribution at all before the twentieth century apart from the probate returns, which may be questioned on a number of important grounds, especially their age-specific nature, the undercounting of working-class assets, and estate duty avoidance and *inter vivos* gifts among the wealthier classes. Land was entirely excluded from the probate returns until the 1890s, while very little data exists in official sources about the distribution of wealth from the probate sources (or any other) until the 1890s at the earliest. What sources do exist, however, overwhelmingly and incontrovertibly suggest that there was a striking degree of inequality in the distribution of wealth in Britain at this time. One of the very few nineteenth-century sources on the distribution of personal property according to the probate returns, published in the Parliamentary Papers in 1861, revealed that 29,979 persons (20,867 men and 9,112 women) left property at death in England and Wales in 1858. But some 227,000 men and 222,000 women (including minors) died in England and Wales in that year. The overwhelming majority of persons – around 80 per cent of all adult men and 90 per cent of all adult women – left *no property at all* passing by probate. Of the total of £69,893,000 represented by these 29,979 estates, just under half, some £33,890,000, was left by precisely 587 persons, and the wealthiest 67 persons left 22 per cent of all property passing at death in 1858 and caught by the probate net.[20] Even if a large fraction of the two hundred thousand or so adults dying in 1858 who left (according to this source) nothing actually left £100 each in property which was outside of the probate net and hence not included in these official statistics – a supposition which is almost certainly a considerable exaggeration of working-class affluence – only £20 million must be added to the £69.9 million passing by probate and which was actually 'caught' by the official statistics. Furthermore, it must not be forgotten that this figure of £69.9 million itself excludes *all land*, and a brief consideration of the effect of taking landed property into account here is enlightening. Landed property was almost certainly far more unequally distributed than personal (i.e. non-landed) property. In 1872, some 33,080,076 acres were owned by private landowners in Britain. Of this total, 23,328,576 acres were owned by just 13,802 larger landowners and yeomen owning 500 or more acres and the remaining 9,751,500 acres by 944,750 smaller landowners and cottagers. These figures exclude land situated in London; taking this into account would doubtless add still further to the degree of inequality (Bateman, 515). An acre of land was usually worth on average £30 or so when sold, and about one-thirtieth of all land-owners – very roughly – would have died in any particular year – suggesting that an additional £33 million (approximately) must be added to the £69.9 million of personal property caught by the landed probate net in 1858. Some £23.3 million of this landed wealth would have been left by about 440 greater landowners (one-thirtieth of 13,802), with just thirteen great landowners leaving £5,729,000. It must also be remembered that these greater land-owners dying in 1858 were *not* different individuals from those caught in the probate net as leaving personal property, but in nearly every case also left substantial personal estates as well. Ten of the sixty-five male estates worth £100,000 or more in personal property in 1858 were, in fact, left by peers, who were mainly great landowners. Thus the number of wealthy individuals leaving substantial estates in 1858 is probably not much greater than the number already caught in the probate net but the true value of their total wealth must be increased by a very large amount; possibly, for (say) all persons leaving £25,000 or more it must be doubled. Even if working-class wealth is brought into these figures, then the missing upper-class landed wealth more than compensates for this addition and makes the total distribution of wealth in mid-Victorian Britain even more uneven than it seems at first glance.

The distribution of wealth in mid-Victorian Britain was certainly more unequal than was the distribution of income at the same time, in all likelihood by a very marked degree. Clearly, if about 80 per cent of all deceased males owned no property at all caught by the probate net, while only 587 persons out of over 200,000 deceased adults left nearly half of the total passing by probate, this suggests a degree of inequality far in excess of any conceivably indicated by an analysis of income distribution. Wealth is in nearly every society and situation more unequally distributed than income, for wealth represents past income which has been accumulated, saved and invested. The majority of the British population, those on the borderline of poverty or below the poverty line, were unable to save anything, even allowing for the enormous differences in incomes which existed. A very disproportionate share of pre-industrial wealth was held in the form of land, which remained in very few hands because of primogeniture, strict settlement, the complex nature of the conveyancing laws, and the Enclosure movement, while land always retained and regularly increased its value down the years, given the pressure of a growing population upon a resource which could never grow. Business, professional and farming income prior to the nineteenth century had few secure outlets for investment besides land (phenomenally expensive to purchase on a large scale) and government securities. The same was true *a fortiori* of the pre-industrial artisan class.

If one asks of the distribution of wealth in the nineteenth century the same questions as were posed earlier of nineteenth-century income distribution, did it become more unequal as a result of industrialization, and when did a trend to more equal distribution begin, one is much less likely to obtain clear-cut or satisfactory answers, both because of the nature of the evidence and the nature of changes in the wealth structure during this period. Because land-owning – the backbone of pre-industrial wealth – was so unequally distributed, it seems implausible to suggest that wealth distribution became more unequal still as a result of industrialization. This might have happened, but only if post-industrial business wealth was even more unequally distributed than pre-industrial landed wealth, or if industrialization further augmented the wealth of landowners to a disproportionate extent, or if the post-industrial working class was relatively larger and poorer than its pre-industrial counterpart.

The Industrial Revolution did not create, and certainly did not immediately create, a new class of super-rich industrialists and entrepreneurs (Rubinstein, 1981, Chapter 3). As we have seen, the number of personal estates of £100,000 or more (including those left by landowners) rose from an annual average of 16.5 in 1809–14 (the first period for which figures are available) to 29.0 in 1825–9, but then only to 31.6 in 1850–4 (Rubinstein, 1981, 34). Nor did the number of millionaires rise by much. Most successful businessmen left estates in the range of £50,000–200,000 or so in this period, and the capital value of even large factories was surprisingly low. Certainly landowners remained virtually unchallenged at the peak of the wealth scale until the later nineteenth century. Indeed, the effect of industrialization and urbanization was further to advantage those landowners – generally, the richest ones – with substantial mineral or urban properties and if wealth did become more unequally distributed in nineteenth-century Britain, it was probably because of this factor rather than because a new class of industrialists came into being.

At the other end of the social scale there was some growth in working-class ownership of property, but not much. As is evident from Table 8 (see p. 87), the overwhelming majority of the working class were renters rather than home owners not only down to 1914 but much later. Working-class savings, as in friendly societies and savings banks, grew steadily especially during the later nineteenth century. As early as 1803 there were 9,672 friendly societies in Britain with 704,350 members (Gosden, 12). Seventeen per cent of the total population of Lancashire were members of a friendly society in 1821, suggesting, it would seem, that well over half of all adult males in Lancashire belonged to one during the apogee of industrialization. By 1877, all of the registered friendly societies had a total membership of 2.75 million, a figure which grew to 5.6 million by 1904. Similarly, the number of depositors in the Post Office Savings Banks grew from 663,000 in 1863–8 to 5.8 million by 1891–5. (Gosden, 11, 12, 91, 139.)

These figures are certainly impressive – and an often neglected facet of industrialization in Britain – but should be seen in perspective: probably 75 per cent (or more) of a British population numbering 22 million in 1851 and 41 million in 1911 may be assigned to the working classes, and the *per capita* savings and property of this majority section of the population were pitifully low. There were clearly many skilled workers in prosperous industries even in the mid-nineteenth century who were able to amass some wealth, and it would seem that their number steadily increased. The father of Labour politician Philip Snowden was probably a typical example of this category of worker. This man, John Snowden, was an ordinary weaver in Cowling, Yorkshire, who left £485, amassed through thrift and savings, at his death in 1889. His wife, it is said, had lived in twenty-one different houses in Yorkshire in the course of her perambulatory working-class life. The son became a minor civil servant and an early Labour Party pioneer, rising, as is well known, eventually to become Chancellor of the Exchequer and a viscount. While such a tale is obviously an extreme example of social mobility, there were certainly thousands of John Snowdens by mid-century. Presumably there were relatively fewer earlier in the century, although the immediate increase in poverty and lower living standards which might have been caused by early industrialization and the rapid increase in population might have brought about a decline in the level of previous property ownership by workers. If such a decline occurred it presumably occurred as a result of a massive shift of very small farmers and agricultural labourers, who enjoyed pre-Enclosure common law 'property' entitlements and who may have owned some livestock and household effects, to the factory towns, where they owned nothing. So far as I am aware, there is no convincing evidence of any such decline, and the impressive growth of the friendly societies and early savings banks just at this time argues against such a notion; furthermore, it should not be forgotten that (contrary to the layman's popular belief) the wages for adult males in factories were considerably higher than those of rural workers.

Nevertheless, pre-industrial Britain was a society where, it is often argued, extremes of wealth *seemed* much less sharp than after industrialization and some minimal property ownership was apparently very widespread, at least outside of London and the remote Celtic areas. One recent historian has estimated that in Oxfordshire in the sixteenth century about two-thirds to three-quarters of the population were worth more than £5 and should, therefore, have made wills or had grants of administration, but as Anthony J. Camp notes 'it seems clear that nothing like this number did' (Camp, xxxvii–xxxviii). However Joan Thirsk found that in one Nottinghamshire parish, in the period 1572–1600, just over one-quarter of the deceased population left wills – an astonishingly high proportion – while in the years 1660–1725 only one-fifth of the deceased population left a will. Nationally in the 1790s the proportion was 6 per cent and by 1873 it was 8 per cent (Camp, xxxviii). Until these numbers are calculated exactly and carefully linked to adult deaths, however, little of a conclusive nature can be said about this indicator of property ownership. It is possible that, broadly, the eighteenth and early nineteenth century saw a diminution in the overall spread of property ownership, but this must remain only a possibility without detailed evidence, and the growth of working-class savings institutions like the friendly societies argues against it, at least tentatively.

There was clearly some increase in the spread of wealth holding and property ownership in the later nineteenth century. As noted, deposits in Post Office Savings Banks, for instance, rose from £1.7 million in 1862 (its first year of operation) to £25.2 million in 1875 to £140.4 million in 1901 and £190.5 million in 1914. On the other hand, by 1900–01, of 343,000 adults who died in England and Wales, 62,523 left some estate caught by the probate, including very small estates – about 18.2 per cent of the population – only marginally higher than in 1858. It seems clear that any realistic opportunities for working-class savings were very limited even at the turn of the century, although they were probably growing slowly.

There also seems little doubt that the number of wealthy persons was growing rapidly, especially in the later nineteenth century. The number of estates of £100,000 or more grew from 53.4 *per annum* in 1860–4 to 185.5 in 1890–3. Thereafter better official statistics are available and they show a smaller rise, from about 265 *per annum* in 1895–9 to 300 *per annum* in 1900–14. Very large fortunes, up to £10 million or more, began to be left by Britain's multi-millionaires, and the Edwardian period has become famous for the display and vulgar behaviour of its wealthy class. For these reasons it is probable that no diminution in the degree of wealth inequality occurred at this time and there was, possibly, an increase in inequality.

The most recent and most comprehensive historian of this subject is the American economic historian Peter H. Lindert, whose research on *income* distribution was discussed above. In his work *Lucrens Angliae: the Distribution of English Private Wealth Since 1760* (which Professor Lindert kindly allowed me to read in manuscript form), several conclusions can be reached from his searching and highly sophisticated data. Concerning the 'distribution of total assets' in England and Wales from successive probate samples between 1740 and the twentieth century, Lindert has noted (p. 53 of the manuscript version):

> As far as the data can reveal, wealth inequality remained steady from 1740 until 1911–13, subject to what are now wide confidence bounds. The pronounced levelling of wealth inequality within this century has left us with a distribution in the 1970s and 1980s that is clearly less unequal than any now documented for the past.

If Lindert is correct, trends in wealth inequality would seem to parallel the strangely inconclusive findings of Table 4 (p. 69) concerning income distribution: industrialization's *net* effects were surprisingly limited, probably because various major trends which affected wealth distribution (capital accumulation, inheritance patterns, landownership, population growth) were pulling in various directions at once, and these tended to cancel each other out. As with the income findings, there seems little doubt that this century has seen a notable trend toward greater equality.

A consistent historical series on wealth distribution, derived from the probate records, is available for England and Wales from 1923 and for Great Britain from 1938. It was compiled by the economists A.B. Atkinson and A.J. Harrison.[21] This is probably the most accurate of a number of similar historical studies which derive essentially from the probate records and, generally, attempt to rework these statistics to take account of 'missing' wealth not caught by the probate returns.[22] Table 9 summarizes the findings of Atkinson and Harrison about the amount of wealth owned by various proportions of the adult population:

TABLE 9: Distribution of wealth, 1924–73
(from Harrison in Jones, ed., 70–1)

Proportion of Adults	1924–30	1936	1951–6	1960	1965	1970	1973
Top 1%	57.7	53.0	40.9	35.1	31.9	28.2	27.4
Top 5%	80.1	77.0	66.7	60.9	56.8	54.0	51.9
Top 10%	87.9	86.0	77.4	73.4	70.3	65.4	64.1
Top 20%	93.6	92.2	83.6	85.0	85.4	81.5	n.a.
Bottom 80%	6.4	7.8	16.4	15.0	14.6	18.5	n.a.

Several striking conclusions are immediately apparent from this table. On this measurement at least, wealth was – and is – distributed in a strikingly uneven manner, much more unevenly than is income, although all the caveats noted earlier about the use of the probate returns for this purpose must be kept squarely in mind. Even in 1973 the top 10 per cent of wealth leavers owned nearly three times as great a proportion of the total national capital as the top 10 per cent of income earners earned of the total national income.

But equally there has been a considerable growth in wealth equalization in Britain since the 1920s, although this redistributionist trend has been much more marked at the *very* top levels, among the top 1 per cent and 5 per cent of wealth holders, than among the top 10 or 20 per cent, let alone the bottom quartiles. This apparent fact has been widely noted by many economists who work in this area, and there has been much comment that the real movement in wealth distribution has been from the very richest to the merely well off. To this day, as noted before, more than half the deceased adult population leaves no property at all at death which is caught by the probate net. As noted previously this is only one of the difficulties of ascertaining the distribution of wealth from the probate returns.

For the most recent period, the Inland Revenue has made its own calculations on the distribution of wealth. These have the great merit of including some (but not all) of the types of wealth not caught by the probate net. In particular they take into account the value of occupational pension rights and state pension rights as well as the value of marketable wealth left at death. Table 10 outlines the distribution of wealth according to the Inland Revenue, showing both the value of marketable wealth alone and after the inclusion of both occupational and state pension rights.

As will be apparent, there has been a rapid shift in the distribution of wealth away from the very richest groups during the most recent decade. Some of this redistribution was caused by the sharp decline in share values – a major part of the portfolios of the very wealthy – during the recession of the early 1970s, and further marked redistribution has not occurred. On the other hand, no marked increase in inequality has occurred either, despite the rise in share and property values and the steady growth of unemployment. Additionally, although the shift away from the very rich appears substantial if

TABLE 10: Distribution of wealth
Inland Revenue statistics, 1971–80[23]

Marketable wealth alone	1971	1974	1978	1979	1980	1981
Top 1%	31	23	23	24	23	23
Top 5%	52	43	44	45	43	45
Top 10%	65	57	58	59	58	60
Top 25%	86	84	83	82	81	84
Top 50%	97	93	95	95	94	94

Marketable wealth plus occupational pension rights						
	1971	1974	1978	1979	1980	1981
Top 1%	27	19	19	20	19	19
Top 5%	46	38	39	38	37	37
Top 10%	59	52	52	51	50	50
Top 25%	78–83	76–82	75–79	75–79	73–77	73–77
Top 50%	90–96	88–92	89–93	89–93	89–93	89–93

Marketable wealth plus occupational and state pension rights						
	1971	1974	1978	1979	1980	1981
Top 1%	21	15	13	13	12	12
Top 5%	37	31	25	27	25	25
Top 10%	49	43	36	37	35	35
Top 25%	69–72	64–67	57–60	58–61	57–60	57–60
Top 50%	85–89	85–89	79–83	79–83	79–83	78–82

only marketable wealth is considered, it is even more dramatic if pension rights are taken into account. Unfortunately for the historian, it does not appear as if any calculations exist previous to the 1960s which take pension rights into account in determining wealth distribution,[24] but it is worth recalling that state pensions did not become universal entitlements until 1946, while the number and range of private pensions must have increased enormously, as a middle-class fringe benefit, since the Second World War.

Although there seems little doubt of a continuing and significant redistribution of wealth away from the very wealthiest portion of the population to the less wealthy majority of the population, the bottom portions of the population have been relatively unaffected – again, the thrust of wealth distribution has been from the very wealthiest to the merely wealthy or affluent sections of the population. It is probable that within a number of decades this is also likely to change in a redistributionist direction, as the great increase in home ownership among younger age groups eventually manifests itself in the appearance of many more substantial estates among an ever growing portion of the population. This will be augmented by the increase in savings and investments among many sections of the population, and in the near ubiquity of privately owned chattels and consumer durables with some market value, like cars and televisions. Some factors which may affect this prediction are any possible increase in the increments in wealth holding among the very wealthiest portions of the population at a considerably faster rate than the general population (in one direction) or (in the other) the introduction of a wide-ranging wealth tax. (In this connection it should be noted that none of the statistics presented in this chapter take the effects of death duties, which are steeply progressive, into account. After the payment of death duties the amount of wealth inherited by the heirs of wealthy persons is considerably less than those figures suggest.) Finally, the effects of high unemployment on a historically high percentage of the population, if it continues for a long period, may well act to increase wealth inequality; certainly any long-term postponement of the now normal acquisitions of a mortgage and personal property will still have an effect many decades hence, especially if such accumulation at a young age is still possible for another, luckier portion of the same generational cohort. On balance, however, there is little doubt that the redistributionist trends evident since 1945 (if not before) will continue for an indefinite period. Comparing the trends of income and wealth distribution it is apparent that the two trends are very similar, with the rates of wealth distribution lagging behind (or following) those of income distribution by some decades. This is precisely what one would expect given the age-specific nature of the probate statistics from which the data of wealth distribution is drawn, for the reasons outlined earlier. Indeed, the rapid increase in wealth redistribution away from the very wealthiest classes is somewhat surprising, given the persistence of wealth concentrations via inheritance and inter-generational gifts. The meagre portion of the wealth cake owned by the poorer half of the population is also likely to alter and increase as post-war growth in home ownership and other widely-owned possessions increasingly affects the probate data. Behind the rhetoric of economic decline which has dominated political debate, from every ideological direction, over the past generation, Britain may have quietly and almost unobserved become in fact another desideratum of popular rhetoric – something like a property-owning democracy, and unequivocally much more like one than it has ever been.

The data presented here, taken in conjunction with the evidence presented earlier on consumer durables and housing tenure, indicates an unprecedented, drastic and relatively sudden improvement in the British standard of living and in equality trends during the very recent past. It takes an effort of the imagination to realize that these trends occurred precisely at the time when, according to virtually all economists and social commentators, and to all of the 'normal' economic indicators, Britain's economic performance has been both worse than at any time since industrialization began and markedly worse than that of any other developed nation. Britain's allegedly unrelenting economic decline forms, of course, the theme of hundreds of books and thousands of editorials written over the past thirty or more years. From the large pile of such books presently on my desk, two absolutely typical descriptions from recent works might be selected to illustrate the burden of such critiques, one by a distinguished economic historian and the other from a work by two economists which received wide publicity when it first appeared (in the *Sunday Times*) during the mid-1970s:

> There are various ways in which these totals of goods and services can be summed . . . How does Britain fare in such comparisons? The statistics confirm the national consciousness of a staggering relative decline, such as would have been considered unbelievable only a little over thirty years ago . . . Within the span of half a lifetime, Britain has descended from the most prosperous major state of Europe to the Western European slum . . . She has become the proverbial failure . . .
>
> There is in operation, we have noticed above, a law of the deterioration of British economic policy . . . With Mr Healey as Chancellor, we seemed to have reached the lowest possible plateau . . . [but] the present [Tory] government has done more damage more rapidly than any previous administration . . . (Pollard, *British Economy*, 2, 6, 165).

★ ★ ★

> Up to June 1970 each administration achieved successes as well as failures . . . What was unique about Mr Heath's 1970–4 administration was that failure was total (Bacon and Ellis, 56).

The glaring incongruity between such critiques – and any among fifty others might have been readily substituted for them – and the statistics presented here seems difficult to accommodate under the normal modes of studying Britain's economic performance, based centrally upon comparative economic growth rates. Arguably, the most frequently employed determinants of economic success *must* be misleading in failing to take into account such important matters as real changes in the standards of living and in the distribution of wealth. It is perhaps for this reason, too, that although political activists and elements of the intelligentsia have moved to much less consensual and centrist positions than has been the case since 1939, most ordinary Englishmen appear to be much more sanguine than their leaders. Nothing said here can, of course, alter the grim reality of life in contemporary Britain faced by an unskilled inner city teenager, a redundant steelworker in Sheffield, or an unemployable dock labourer in Liverpool, but despite all the seeming evidence to the contrary such groups form a minority amongst a majority whose living standards are incontestably rising, probably more markedly than at any time in British history.

Further, although the middle classes have of course benefited disproportionately from the rise in living standards, to a surprising extent these determinants of living standards have been shared in by the entire population. Obviously, if 93 per cent of all households now own a refrigerator (see Table 7), the great majority of working-class households must own one. When these consumer durables are not today almost universally owned, the key determinant of ownership appears to be age as much as social class, with fewer among the elderly nearly always owning such items than younger households. Although this of course reflects the decreased earning capacity of the elderly, as noted above, it is also a product of their differing social mores and, often, the inappropriateness of possessing an item like a car – owned by only 32 per cent of elderly households, compared with 72 per cent of households with children. With the all-important factor of housing tenure, however, there is clear evidence of the spread of wealth ownership throughout nearly all of the population. The 1983 edition of *Social Trends* has an important table on this matter (see Table 11).

As will be seen, among households with an economically active head, only among the bottom two groups, accounting for only 12.9 per cent of the population, are less than one-half of

TABLE 11: Tenure of households, by socio-economic group of head of households, 1981, by percentages[25]

Socio-economic Group of Household Head & Percentage of Total	Owner-Occupied			Rented	
	Owned Outright	Owned with Mortgage	Local Authority/ New Town	Unfurnished Private	Furnished Private
Professional, Employers, Managers	15.4	20	62	8	7	3
Intermediate Non-manual	5.8	17	60	12	5	5
Junior Non-manual	7.4	17	49	20	9	4
Skilled Manual & Own Account Non-Professional	22.4	16	42	33	7	1
Semi-Skilled and Personal service	10.0	14	27	44	12	3
Unskilled	2.9	15	16	57	9	2
Economically Inactive Head	36.2	40	4	42	12	2

the total owner occupiers; and even then two-fifths of the semi-skilled households own or are purchasing their homes (41 per cent). Among skilled households, 58 per cent own or are buying their homes. Only the fact that only 44 per cent of households with economically inactive heads (mainly the elderly) own their own homes prevents the overall percentage of home ownership in Britain from exceeding 60 per cent. Among households headed by economically active heads, nearly 64 per cent owned or were buying their homes in 1981.

The reasons for the rise in home ownership (and, as a result, property ownership) in recent years are difficult to pinpoint. Relative to real incomes, it is doubtful that house prices have fallen compared with the situation in the 1930s or even the 1950s; on the contrary, house prices in the south-east have escalated dramatically and in London, astronomically, since the early 1960s. Similarly, interest rates have risen sharply. Probably three factors have most accounted for the rise in home ownership: a marked increase in the number of two-income households, the much greater availability of mortgage finance, and, more subtly, the rising expectations and changing values among the working classes and lower middle classes for an affluent lifestyle, demands which somehow have transmitted themselves into securing the means to make this possible, and the channelling of personal economic gains made via economic growth and trade union action into savings rather than consumption. One probable indication of the importance of the last of these factors may be seen in the fact that the post-war growth in home ownership and the possession of consumer durables has proceeded apparently without interruption or variation under governments of left and right and during every sort of economic circumstances. The 1950s saw the largest relative rise in home ownership, but this has continued as well under all subsequent Labour governments. At the present time British rates of consumer durable ownership are increasingly comparable to those in the United States (while for most consumer durables there is probably no difference between the 'sick' economy of Britain and the relatively 'healthy' economies of western Europe), and levels of home ownership will probably soon approach the 65–70 per cent level found in countries like Australia and America. These trends, it should be reiterated, have occurred at just the time when the more usual indices of economic development have recorded an apparently unrelieved decline in Britain's economic performance. Similarly, and probably related to this, it seems clear that an increasing proportion of the working population has become linked for the first time to the banking system. As recently as 1969, 75 per cent of *all* workers in Britain were paid by cash, 15 per cent by direct transfer to a bank account, and only 10 per cent by cheque. By 1981, the respective percentages of these types of payment were 44, 42, and 14 per cent.[26] In 1981, 61 per cent of the adult British population had a bank account of some kind, while only 15 per cent still had no form of savings account (including building societies, Girobank, etc.).[27] Once again, the pattern seems to be that there has been a remarkable and unprecedented spread through the whole population of financial habits which were, only a decade or two before, the preserve of the middle classes, again at a time of economic distress.

Of course, as everybody knows, there is certainly another side to this picture. The paradox of the contemporary British economy lies in the fact that side by side with unprecedented gain have occurred rates of unemployment unparalleled since the Depression, unemployment in Britain rising sharply from only 5.3 per cent in 1979 to 10.5 per cent in 1981, 12.2 per cent in 1982, and 13.0 per cent in September 1983, stabilizing at between 12 and 13 per cent since then. The pointless and immense human cost and waste cannot be conveyed by these figures, nor can the gloom of the depressed industrial town or the lost generation of school leavers. Rates of unemployment nearly as high, and occasionally higher, prevailed throughout much of western Europe, and it is clear that the shift of skilled manufacturing industry to the rim of east Asia since the 1970s may well have long-term consequences for the countries of Europe as great as a major war.

Despite any of this, all of the quantitative statistics of wealth holding suggest that overall the picture is highly sanguine, and that these changes have important political consequences is widely acknowledged. Many clear-eyed Conservative thinkers have seen the real spread of property ownership throughout the whole population as a major key to electoral success. Although this may be debated – the most important long-term political hallmark of the post-1955 period has been the decline of *both* the Tory and Labour votes at the expense of third parties – it seems clearly in the interest of Conservative governments to create the circumstances under which most personal incomes will grow sufficiently to allow the widespread purchase of property with a market value, especially housing, rather than remain so small that only the purchase of life's necessities is possible for the majority of people. Conservative governments might, indeed, reconsider the wisdom of routinely opposing all 'outrageous' wage claims by trade unions: in the long term it is the spread of affluence to all which weakens socialism. This is especially true if, as has been suggested, the more usual indicators of economic performance do not really come to terms with accurately measuring living standards.

The spread of an affluent society alone cannot, of course, guarantee the success of conservatism; indeed, if there has been any determinable political response at all, it has been in the growth of the radical but non-socialist centre-left parties, the Liberals and the Social Democrats, who are possibly strongest among what used to be termed the 'Orpington' type of young couple with a mortgage.*

---

*'Orpington' refers to a celebrated by-election in 1962 won by the Liberals from the ruling Conservatives; Orpington was widely seen to be inhabited by many young couples of this type.

What seems indisputable, however, is that the long-term prospects of the Labour Party have, at least through the 1983 Election, steadily declined, a trend which Labour theorists have increasingly linked to the development of substantial working-class property ownership. Two recent articles in *New Socialist*, the theoretical Labour monthly, have expressed these doubts. Professor John Westergaard noted:

> Promoted by the more or less enthusiastic policies of successive governments, owner occupation of housing has so spread – unlike ownership of business capital – that by 1981 well over half of all households 'headed' by skilled manual or junior non-manual workers owned or were buying their homes . . . The broad effect has been to produce a new dividing line among people dependent on 'jobs' [*sic*]: home ownership brings some real economic advantage.
>
> While a total reversal of policy in this field is inconceivable, it may not be too late for new initiatives – towards occupancy of both private and council housing on long leaseholds with freehold reversion to public hands . . . (Westergaard, 34).

The problem with such a proposal is that if it were seriously taken up by the Labour Party – if it were seriously proposed, for instance, to convert existing freeholds into long-term leaseholds which revert at some stage to 'public hands' – the Labour Party would surely suffer an electoral defeat of a magnitude which would make 1983 seem like a slight downturn of fortunes. Reviewing a book on the growth of owner occupation, Labour researcher David Griffiths explained that Labour's left

> has seen the rise of owner occupation as a negative development. It is seen as 'functional' for capital – and thus damaging to the Labour movement – in at least two important ways. It sustains the ideology of private capital; and it fragments the working class into 'housing classes' of owners and tenants with conflicting positions (Griffiths, 60).

Griffiths contrasts this perception with the attitude of Labour's right wing, which has welcomed the spread of owner occupation, and, indeed, the apparent contradictions in Labour's attitude toward home ownership may be one of their central conceptual weaknesses at the present time. Some Labour spokesmen seem to come close to suggesting that the British working class has become too affluent, and ought to be restored to poverty.

Finally, the growth of widespread property ownership will have its effects upon future generations, as more and more people inherit substantial amounts of money. Even now, only about half of the deceased population leaves any property counted for probate purposes, but this proportion is bound to rise continuously as the newly-propertied age and die off. Concomitantly, the truly property-less are bound to decline as a proportion of the population, and become largely confined to those households with 'multiple problems' or plain bad luck. Interestingly, it appears that many non-white migrants are sharing in the growth of property ownership. In 1981, the percentage of households headed by an Indian/Pakistani/ Bangladeshi either owning or purchasing their own homes was actually considerably *higher* than the equivalent percentage of households headed by 'whites' (75 per cent as against 55 per cent), while such households headed by a member of other non-European groups, apart from West Indians, amounted to 41 per cent of the total in this category, with 27 per cent living as tenants of local authorities and 30 per cent privately renting. Only among West Indian/Guyanese households was there a relative failure to attain widespread property ownership. Even here, 37 per cent of all British blacks owned or were purchasing their own homes, a higher percentage than among all British households as recently as 1956.[28] The high proportion of West Indian households outside of the network of property ownership might well be a more salient explanatory variable for the allegedly high figures of antisocial behaviour among this group, in areas like street crimes and family breakdowns, than many other explanations which have been offered and should, in my view, occupy the attention of researchers. Similarly, regional differentiations in property ownership to the detriment of Northern Ireland and Scotland (where nearly 60 per cent of all households live in council houses) might also be usefully studied in this context.[29]

These gains in property ownership continued, so far as the statistics will bear this out, during the severe recession of 1979–82. Indeed, the rate of increase in, for instance, ownership of consumer durables would have been seen as remarkable a decade or two before, but has been largely ignored amid the general gloom and the tacit expectation of continuing failure. Households with telephones, for instance, rose from 45 per cent in 1973 to 67 per cent in 1979 to 76 per cent in 1982. Similarly, the percentage of all British households with such consumer durables as washing machines (up from 75 to 79 per cent), tumble driers (up from 19 to 26 per cent), central heating (52 to 60 per cent), and colour televisions (61 to 77 per cent) also rose continuously during the worst recession in fifty years. So far as the statistics indicate, for no type of consumer durable did the 'percentage of owning households' decline, and, yet again, the rate of gain during this period was as high as, or higher, than during times of affluence and full employment in the past.[30]

III

The pattern of income
and wealth inequality
in Britain: interpretations

Merely broadly to outline the historical trends in wealth and income distribution is not to explain why they occurred. That is the task of this section. Cogently and comprehensively to explain any historical phenomenon is difficult enough, but it is especially difficult in accounting for historical trends in British income and wealth distribution. Very broad periods, which encompassed fundamental economic and social changes like industrialization, must necessarily be examined. The quantitative evidence is, as we have repeatedly seen, rather poor, with lengthy gaps in our knowledge, approximations, and simple guesswork the rule more often than not until the contemporary era.

Furthermore, it is important to bear in mind that there is really no way to assess the relative importance of the various factors which may be suggested as influencing trends in wealth and income distribution. It is possible, indeed likely, that major influences on these trends worked in opposite ways at once. For example, to take one apparently straightforward (or is it?) example of such a cross-current of influence, sustained economic growth from 1760 to 1870 was probably cancelled out by unprecedented population growth (or was it?), and the changes in income or wealth distribution in this period may be seen as the product of two influences pulling in opposite directions; additionally, there were whatever contemporaneous or long-term influences the historian might wish to adduce – the effects of the Napoleonic Wars or the two World Wars, structural changes in employment, the trade unions, tariffs and government policies to name only a few. With such a bewildering array of possible contributory effects upon the direction of income distribution, it seems almost impossible accurately to pinpoint the responsibility of each factor for the outcome and its changes down the years. Finally, historians have seemingly devoted little attention to this question compared with many other areas of economic history. Perhaps the one sustained historical debate which bears on this area, the question of the working-class standard of living during industrialization, is notorious for its inconclusive nature and, especially, for its lack of clarity between qualitative and quantitative evidence.

Having said this, it is now necessary to consider the main historical factors which have contributed to significant changes in the distribution of wealth and income in Britain. It is probably useful to divide these into long-term factors, which are independent of particular historical events or government acts, and short-term factors:

Long-term factors
- economic growth
- employment shifts from the primary to the secondary to the tertiary sectors
- the effects of capitalism as an economic system
- regional population trends
- population growth
- employment/unemployment
- trends in the availability of finance
- 'psychological equality' and the spread of middle-class aspirations
- education
- inheritance patterns

Short-term factors
- the effects of trade unions and industrial action
- the effect of wars
- taxation policies
- deliberate government measures of redistribution; the 'Welfare State'

Economic growth

The search for the causes of sustained economic growth – that is, a continuing (over the long term) increase in a nation's total income – is perhaps the main concern of contemporary economists, while many economic historians view the essence of the Industrial Revolution *as* the introduction of continuing economic growth into a nation's economy.

In itself, the mere fact of sustained economic growth (such as Britain has experienced since industrialization) or even the absence of sustained economic growth – has no necessary implications for the distribution of income and wealth. It is not only quite possible to imagine increasing inequality as occurring simultaneously with the beginnings of sustained economic growth via industrialization, but this may well be the rule, as Kuznets (above, p. 59) has suggested. In many cases, the resources for investment during industrialization must come from short-term sacrifices in wages; the newly-rich entrepreneurs thrown up by industrialization and the landowners who may incidentally profit from it are likely, in a capitalist society, to become relatively wealthier and to earn a larger share of the national cake; the converse of this process, the creation of an urban proletariat, may add further to income maldistribution.

Nevertheless, in the long term it is likely that sustained economic growth *per se* is a significant contributory factor to increasing equalities in the distribution of wealth and income. There are several reasons for this. In the first place, sustained economic growth at a rate *faster* than population growth at least makes possible a more equal distribution of incomes, while the absence of economic growth, if accompanied by population growth, is a near certain recipe for economic and even demographic disaster (as in nineteenth-century Ireland). It is largely for this reason that in today's poorest Third World countries there is probably a more unequal structure of income and wealth in, say, those Asian countries experiencing rapid growth; certainly such areas as Hong Kong, Singapore, and South Korea seem to have a better chance of avoiding the chronic rural backwardness and misery of a Bangladesh or the equally chronic underemployment and hopelessness of the new urban ghettoes found, say, throughout Latin America.

There are, however, further reasons why economic growth may well lead to a more equal distribution of income and wealth. Under capitalism economic growth can be sustained only if entrepreneurs can sell their goods; while they may export much of what they produce, in general the vigorous demand created by a growing home economy is a more important factor than the export market. (There is a lively debate among economic historians as to which was the more significant in 'triggering' Britain's economic takeoff, the domestic market or foreign exports.) Thus, though business does possess an obvious vested interest in keeping wages and labour costs low, it equally requires sufficient domestic demand for a buoyant market, and businessmen are not necessarily averse to rising working-class incomes and certainly not to a rising national income – indeed, without a prosperous market their businesses will necessarily be less successful. Many economic historians believe that the fact that Britain *already* had the most prosperous working class in Europe by 1750 was a key factor in why industrialization occurred first in Britain and not in France or the Netherlands; Victorian prosperity was built upon a working class far better off than Europe's peasantries or relatively small class of urban workers; in more recent times, not all businessmen, or even many, have opposed governmental measures of fiscal management designed to produce economic growth and relatively full employment. It may be that a continuously prospering working class – implying a redistribution of income away from the business classes – is more directly in the interest of these classes than a sharply unequal distribution of the cake.

It may also be argued that continuing economic growth has another important effect upon the (as it were) willpower of the wealthier classes to resist demands (such as trade union actions) by poorer sections of the population for a greater share of the cake. The wealthier sections of the population may well be less willing to resist *à l'outrance* working-class demands for social reforms if their own continuing affluence, albeit rising at a lower rate, is assured. Something of the sort appears to have occurred in many post-1945 Western societies, with conservative and middle-class parties at least acquiescing in far-reaching social legislation of a kind considered intolerable before 1939.

Finally, continuing economic growth is intimately bound up with population growth and family size, a matter to be more fully discussed below. For a variety of reasons, continuing economic growth makes possible smaller families, which in turn raises the living standards of the next and subsequent generations.

Capitalism

Economic growth can and has occurred in many kinds of economic systems. Britain's industrialization took place in only one particular economic system, the system known as capitalism. Does capitalism *per se* contribute anything to the shape of income and wealth inequality? The answer to this is, of course, first and foremost a matter of how one defines 'capitalism', especially in its historical context – when, for instance, did English 'feudalism' end and English 'capitalism' take hold? At the other chronological extreme is the post-1945 British Welfare State economy still essentially capitalistic? Nevertheless, assuming that the British economy for most of the modern period can be described as capitalistic, does this fact in itself contribute to the inequalities which historians have found?

It is plainly true that in a society whose hallmarks are private property ownership, entrepreneurial rewards and profits, and the inheritance of wealth, income and wealth are unlikely to be as equally distributed as in a thorough-going socialist system where accumulations of privately held wealth are impermissible, where there are no large privately owned businesses and the state is the only significant employer of labour. To Marxist critics of British society, there is no doubt that inequality is an all-pervasive and ineradicable feature of capitalism, with the 'ruling class' continuously attempting to 'reproduce' its advantages and, wherever possible, to diminish wages to the subsistence level. The gains which have undoubtedly occurred during the past century in working-class incomes are due, according to this critique, to Britain's imperialist and neo-colonialist exploitation of the tropical world and to the militancy of Britain's trade unions; in any case the levelling process has been exaggerated and significant wealth ownership is still mainly in the hands of a tiny number of large corporations and wealthy capitalists who dominate all Tory governments and, to a surprising extent, all previous Labour governments as well. The educational and cultural system of British society and its pervasive materialistic value system act to perpetuate the capitalist system and its inequalities, even if the working classes (if in employment at all) now possess (because of a century of labour militancy) incomes above the subsistence level.

This, the familiar Marxist critique of British capitalism, represents a consistent but closed world view which attempts cogently to explain the development of all modern societies and is thus nearly impossible either to refute or confirm: one either accepts Marxism's presupposition or one doesn't.

To a considerable extent, the British working class – 75 per cent of the population – remained propertyless and nearly impoverished until very recently; the wealthy and business classes have un-questionably resisted working-class demands for higher wages, while trade unions have come into existence to secure benefits for their members – these facts are undeniable. Beyond this, however, many questions may be asked of a Marxist theory of British capitalism. Would standards of living not have been much higher had not industrialization been accompanied by unprecedented population growth? Do not entrepreneurs have a direct interest in creating an affluent market as well as in keeping wages low? Were there not thoroughly capitalist societies, like the United States and Australia, where working-class living standards were much higher than in Britain? Has not much of the intelligentsia, far from reflecting the 'hegemony' of capitalist values, acted as a perpetual fifth column subversive of 'ruling class' values? Is not the historical pattern of income distribution identified by Kuznets applicable to most industrial societies, regardless of economic system? Finally, how does one explain or account for the seeming sweeping change in the distribution of income and property found during the past thirty years?

Apart from the matter of population growth, the last two points here seem to be the most significant. It may be that income distribution in all societies must become more unequal in the initial stages of industrialization, during the period of heavy investment in industry and in all infrastructure suitable for a modern society. In socialist societies no less than capitalist societies, working-class incomes must necessarily suffer during this period, such as existed classically in Stalinist Russia. It is only later generations prospering from the hard work and sacrifices of their predecessors whose living standards rise markedly. As to the evidence of increasing post-war equality and property ownership among the British working classes, this seems thoroughly at variance with the Marxist critique of British capitalism and its development. The fact that these gains have occurred in one of the West's weakest economies makes the picture even more curious.

Population growth

Again and again we have found a factor of apparently considerable importance in determining the distribution of wealth and income to be population growth. The growth of population in Britain has –

very broadly – followed a two-stage evolution during the past 200 years: an enormous increase (despite massive emigration abroad), absolutely without precedent in British or indeed human history, from about 1760 to 1900 or so, followed thereafter by a much slower rate of population growth, including some periods, such as the 1930s and 1970s, with virtually no population growth at all. If these trends are counterpoised against the long-term trends of economic growth in Britain, it will be seen that the equalizing trend in income distribution which some historians see as having begun in the late nineteenth century began and gathered pace at just the same time as population growth began to level off, while the enormous economic growth experienced by Britain during industrialization was possibly not transformed into a general increase in the standard of living or in income equality because of the equally enormous growth in population.

By decade since the first decennial census was taken in 1801, the percentage increase of population in England and Wales has been as follows:

TABLE 12: Percentage increase of population in England and Wales by decades, 1801–1981

1801–11	14.0	1891–1901	12.2
1811–21	18.1	1901–11	10.9
1821–31	15.8	1911–21	4.9
1831–41	14.3	1921–31	5.5
1841–51	12.7	1931–51*	9.5
1851–61	11.9	1951–61	5.4
1861–71	13.2	1961–71	5.6
1871–81	14.4	1971–81	0.8
1881–91	11.7		

*Because of the Second World War, no census was taken in 1941.

Apart from its likely effect on overall trends in income distribution – where an association can be suggested but not proven – there is the specific and differential effect which trends in population growth had on the incomes of families of different social classes. In particular from the 1870s onwards the number of children produced by the typical middle-class household in Britain declined steadily, although fertility among middle-class households had previously been just as high as among the working classes. In contrast, working-class family size remained very high for many decades to come. This decline in middle-class household size has generally been linked to the late marriages commonly found in many middle-class professions, to the increasing use of birth control, changing perceptions of women's roles and, most significantly, to the rapidly rising costs entailed in bringing up a large middle-class family, especially housing costs and private school fees (Banks (1954), *passim* and (1981), 46–74). Increasingly, in other words, middle-class families were unwilling to sacrifice their higher standard of living by producing more than the number of new mouths to feed requisite for continuing the family's existence; this trend was augmented by the decline in infant and childhood mortality, which ensured that fewer children had to be produced to guarantee the survival to adulthood of a few. By the early part of the present century, this phenomenon had been widely noted by statisticians and led to much comment on the abler classes 'breeding themselves out', accompanied by an undesirable relative increase in the proportion of the less talented working classes, much in keeping with the Darwinian presuppositions of the time.[1] By 1911, the number of children born to families of the different social classes declined steadily as one ascended the social classes, and ranged from 3.99 per family among unskilled labourers to 2.49 per family among the solid middle class (T.H.C. Stevenson, 414).

One effect of this social class differential in family size was further to widen the already enormous gaps in income between the social classes. Working-class families from 1870 to the post-1945 period not merely had less money than middle-class families, they had to divide their incomes among more mouths. Furthermore, social legislation, universal education, and changing patterns of employment increasingly meant that children below ten or twelve (and unlike the earliest phases of industrialization) could not legally be employed, and were simply a deficit to the meagre family budget. Even this assumes, moreover, that each working-class family contained an adult in employment: before the Welfare State, unemployment often meant the workhouse or a life of crime.

Given these differences between typical middle-class and working-class household sizes, it is surprising that income distribution in Britain began to narrow from the 1860s onward – or put perhaps more cogently – if an ostensible narrowing in income distribution between the classes began at that time, this may be rather illusory if differences in typical family size are taken into account. Writing in 1920 of statistics from the 1911 Census, T.H.C. Stevenson made the point that

> the difference in fertility between the social classes is small for marriages contracted before 1861, and rapidly increases to a maximum for those of 1891–96. The slight subsequent approximation between the classes may be apparent rather than real (T.H.C. Stevenson, 431).

Stevenson also noted that the difference in childhood mortality between the social classes, with far more middle-class children surviving proportionally than working-class children, narrowed this gap, but not enough to affect the outcome in a basic way.

One of the major changes which has occurred during the post-1945 period has been a general decline in family size among all social classes, including the working classes. This may probably be viewed as a concealed, but significant, source of further equalization; to this must be added the proliferation of Welfare State measures and especially the great increase in educational opportunities at the secondary and tertiary level. There seems little doubt, however, that very large families are still mainly found among the very poor, and that where such large families exist, this alone is a factor of considerable importance in creating and maintaining poverty. Yet the passage of time, combined with social mores and values differing widely from the past, has certainly diminished the importance of family size. Nor at a macro-level should it be forgotten that the very low rate of British population growth during the past generation (and, comparatively, during this century) has meant that any rise in national product would go relatively much further than during a similar (or greater) period of economic growth accompanied by a rapid increase in population. Indeed, the decline in family size in this century should not be overlooked when putting Britain's relatively very low rate of economic growth in some sort of comparative perspective, especially the paradoxical features we found earlier.

Economic historians often argue that the unexampled growth of population between 1760 and 1900 acted as a spur to economic growth, by enabling a proportion of the labour force to leave the old ways and work in factories, by stimulating demand and markets, and spurring innovation via the increase in younger age cohorts. If this be true, it is widely believed that the population explosion of the eighteenth century was a material factor in triggering a sustained industrial revolution. It is possible that the long-term levelling off in British population growth since 1870 has adversely affected British economic growth during the past century and has been a major contributory factor to its chronically low growth rate, although in this century (and throughout the Western world) there seems to have been a positive correlation between periods of relatively high population growth and economic booms (above all the 1946–73 years). But one of the characteristics of British economic growth in this century and especially in the post-1945 period was that it was generally maintained at a level similar to Britain's long-term growth rate in the past without the stimulus provided by rapid population growth. Clearly, other factors, especially the ever greater demand provided by an increasingly consumer oriented society, have compensated for lower rates of population growth. Rapidly increasing population may, of course, be grossly disadvantageous to economic growth, or to an increase in *per capita* income, as the example of much of the Third World today makes abundantly clear, and the weight of evidence suggests that working-class incomes began to rise only as population growth levelled off.

Sectoral shifts in occupation

A number of other factors, often overlooked in accounting for shifts in income distribution, ought now to be considered. What these have in common with such factors as changes in the rate of population growth is that they have occurred, as it were, exogenously: that is, without any deliberate direction on the part of the state or as a result of purposeful human action, but as part of a 'natural' evolution of the economic system over time. One of the most significant of these is the long-term sectoral shifts in occupation of the labour force from the primary (agriculture) to the secondary (manufacturing and industry) to the tertiary (services, commerce, and the professions) sectors over the past 200 years. In each case the shift in occupational sector resulted in the movement of a substantial percentage of the labour force from a *lower-paid* to a *higher-paid* occupational field over a period of decades, agricultural workers being relatively less well paid than the manufacturing working class, and blue collar workers relatively less well paid than white collar workers. Put another way, the employment growth areas in the British economy over the past 200 years have been relatively better paid than those areas of declining employment activity. Perhaps the best way to demonstrate this is to set out first, the percentage of all males in the labour force from 1841 (the date of the earliest usable census figures)[2] to 1951 employed in the fields of agriculture, horticulture, and forestry (grouped together in the Census classifications). It should be noted that the workers in the agricultural trade would probably include farmers (considered to be middle-class) and even landowners, but the bulk of those listed here would be agricultural labourers.

TABLE 13: Percentage of males in the labour force employed in agriculture and related trades, 1841–1951

1841	28.2%
1851	27.3%
1861	24.5%
1871	20.0%
1881	17.2%
1891	14.2%
1901	11.6%
1911	11.1%
1921	9.8%
1931	8.7%
1951	7.1%

Source: Mitchell and Deane, 60–1. Percentages refer to the total of occupied males.

The clear and steady decline in the percentage of the agricultural sector is striking. Equally, however, it should also be noted that Britain differed from virtually every European country in that there was never a time, at least since the early modern period, when 80–90 per cent of the population was resident in the countryside, as was the case even in France during the nineteenth century. Wages among agricultural labourers were and are among the very lowest in the whole labour force, with a typical weekly wage rate being 8s–10s during the nineteenth century, compared with 18s–25s or even more for skilled adult male factory operatives (Perkin, *Origins* 147–55; Bowley and Hogg, 50). Although these low rates of pay were supplemented by payments in kind and, sometimes, cottage housing, they were still strikingly lower than for most adult male factory hands. John Burnett noted that 'this was a population existing permanently on the verge of starvation' (Burnett, 28). Nor is the situation much changed today, despite some rural unionization, with general farm workers earning an average of £80.10 per week in 1980, the very lowest weekly wage rate of any occupation (Cappelli, 138, 228).

In itself, the historical shift of much of the working class from the countryside to the new factory towns served to *increase* workingclass wages substantially. For those whose image of industrialization is that of the replacement of an idyllic Maypole/Morris dancing rural life by dark satanic mills, it may be hard to believe that such an increase occurred, but nonetheless it did. This is not to say that the nineteenth-century factory towns were pleasant, inviting places – they weren't – or that the routine and repetitive life of a factory operative (to say nothing of a coal miner) was anything but sheer drudgery. But from the viewpoint of earnings, industrial life represented a substantial improvement on rural life. Indeed, the higher wage rates prevailing in the factories might be seen as a kind of bribe to lure unwilling workers into unpleasant employment.

As is well known, many historians and other social commentators (starting with Marx) on Britain's industrialization did not view the fate of the working class in this light but would point to a decline in the working-class standard of living at least until 1850, and a drastic decline in the unquantifiable but all-important quality of workingclass life. About this perspective two things might be said. First, as we have repeatedly seen, it ignores the unprecedented increase in population for whom employment had to be found. Secondly, the classical new industrial working class employed in factories and mines as a result of industrialization was only a minority of the total labour force. Because of the difficulties in assessing the statistics, precise quantification is somewhat misleading, but it appears that in 1861 2,454,000 males out of 7,271,000 in the labour force – only 33.8 per cent – were employed in the classical industries of the industrial revolution.[3] The remainder were employed in commerce, in agriculture, or in small-scale industries. Nor were all of even the 33.8 per cent workers in factories or mines in the accepted sense. Given what has been said about the relatively higher wage rates prevailing in the new industries, it might well be said that the chronic problem with the working-class standard of living during industrialization was not that there was too much of an Industrial Revolution but that there was too little. Britain's industrialization, though it continued apace, was never rapid enough truly to transform the country into an industrial society until the very end of the nineteenth century, if then. Many workers remained sidetracked in dying, unmechanized trades and occupations, while London, with its chronic underemployment and lack of factory industry, remained as much the largest city in Britain in 1914 as in 1760.

This century has seen a new style in the industrial evolution of Britain, with *relatively* better paid white collar workers growing enormously at the expense of manual employment, as the following figure makes clear:

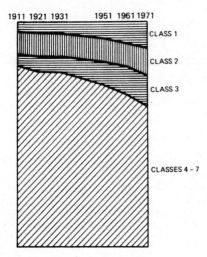

Figure 3 Occupational distribution, 1911–71[4]

These figures apply to males and females. If males alone are considered, the change is even clearer, as Table 14 indicates.

As this table shows, better paid white collar jobs have risen steadily as a percentage of all occupied males. There is one exception to this pattern. The number of *employers* has declined, probably reflecting a drop in the numbers of independent small shopkeepers. Not merely has the working class declined as a percentage of the total male labour force, but, in particular, semi-skilled and (since 1931) unskilled labour has declined *vis-à-vis* the skilled manual categories.

TABLE 14: Percentages of male occupied population by occupational status, 1911–71

			1911	1931	1951	1971
I	a.	Professionals – Higher	1.3	1.5	2.6	4.9
	b.	Professionals – Lower	1.6	2.0	3.2	6.0
2	a.	Employers	7.7	7.7	5.7	5.1
	b.	Managers/Admin	3.9	4.5	6.8	10.9
3		Clerical Workers	5.5	5.5	6.4	6.4
4		Foremen, Supervisors	1.8	2.0	3.3	5.0
5		Skilled Manual	33.0	30.0	30.4	29.1
6		Semi-Skilled Manual	33.6	28.9	27.9	20.8
7		Unskilled Manual	11.6	17.9	13.8	11.9

Source: Routh, 6–7

Although Guy Routh's invaluable work on *Occupation and Pay in Great Britain, 1906–79* does not present similarly authoritative census data for any year more recent than 1971, it does summarize a New Earnings Survey sample taken among one full-time employee in 136 in 1979, as well as a similar previous sample from 1973. The occupational definitions employed in these samples were *not* strictly comparable with the census data presented in Table 14, but they are close enough to indicate continuing trends:

TABLE 15: Percentages of full-time male employees, aged 21 or over, NES samples, 1973 and 1979

		1973	1979
1	Professions	13.4%	15.7%
2	Managers and Administrators	13.4%	16.4%
3	Clerks	6.7%	5.9%
4	Foremen	7.0%	6.9%
Manual Workers			
5	Skilled	19.3%	19.2%
6	Semi-skilled	19.8%	19.1%
7	Unskilled	5.8%	4.7%
Manual	Unclassified	14.6%	12.1%

Source: Routh, 45

Routh notes that 'managers and administrators [were] the fastest growing group', increasing by 22.4 per cent in total number between 1973 and 1979, while manual workers fell by 9.6 per cent between these two years (Routh, 11). Manual workers accounted for 59.5 per cent of all male employees in 1973 but only 55 per cent in 1979. With the severe recession, especially in manufacturing, since 1979, these trends have presumably continued, probably at a faster rate. It is likely that white collar workers are now a majority among the male full-time work force. If full-time women workers are taken into account, white collar workers comprised a majority in 1978 (Routh, 11).

Although this long-term increase in relatively well paying employment at the expense of poorly paying work has been a major factor in the 'levelling up' of incomes, the differential between white collar and blue collar jobs has narrowed steadily from the pre-1914 period to the present, perhaps in line with the levelling of wealth and income discussed earlier. As Table 16 indicates, in 1913–14 Social Class 1A (higher professional) males received on average 2.3 times the average pay of all male workers. By 1978 this had declined to only 1.59 times the average; at the other end of the scale, the pay of unskilled workers had moved upward by nearly 50 per cent.

TABLE 16: Average pay for each men's occupational class expressed as a percentage of the simple average for all men

Class	1913–14	1922–4	1935–6	1955–6	1960	1970	1978
1A	230	206	220	191	195	155	159
1B	109	113	107	75	81	100	104
2B	140	169	153	183	177	180	154
3	69	64	67	65	65	71	71
4	86	95	95	97	97	88	90
5	74	64	68	77	76	76	83
6	48	44	46	58	56	68	73
7	44	45	45	54	51	61	65
All	100	100	100	100	100	100	100
Average £	142·8	283·2	288·1	808·0	1042·5	1887·7	5216·0
% mean deviation	45	47	45	43·5	43·5	34	29

It should also be noted that the very recent rise in the percentage of the population owning their own homes and some property has far exceeded the broad increase in the percentage of middle-class occupations. It has also far exceeded the rise in other socio-economic factors which are strongly linked with, and 'cause' middle-class status, especially education. For instance, the percentage of 17-year-olds receiving a full-time education in Britain rose from 2 per cent of this age group in 1902 only to 4 per cent in 1938, 15 per cent in 1962, and 20 per cent in 1970 (Butler and Sloman, 278). Similarly, although there has been a vast expansion in the tertiary system over the past thirty-five years, in 1982 still only 13.4 per cent of 18-year-olds were receiving a full-time education. This represents a major increase even from 1966 (when only 8.5 per cent were receiving a full-time education), but clearly indicates that the growth of property ownership, and the levelling of income in-equalities, has not been wholly reliant on this pathway of social mobility.

Somewhat similar to this broad historical movement of employ-ment from low paid to well paid trades has been another 'invisible' movement of much the same sort, the geographical shift of popu-lation in Britain since industrialization. It is perhaps insufficiently appreciated that the Industrial Revolution triggered a massive rearrangement of population within Britain. Not only did Lanca-shire's population rise from 673,000 in 1801 to 4,373,000 in 1911, but the relative percentage of Lancashire in the total population of England and Wales rose from 7.57 to 13.20 per cent during the same period. At the other extreme, the population of Cornwall stood at 192,000 (2.16 per cent of the total of England and Wales) in 1801, but only 328,000 (0.91 per cent) in 1911. Regional wage differences in Britain were extremely pronounced at the time. Although industrialization strongly favoured the growth of popu-lation in relatively high wage areas like much of London and Lancashire, many regions of relatively low wages remained strong (Hunt, 7–60). In this century, and especially the past fifty years, there has been a steady shift of population to the more affluent south and away from the old industrial areas of the north, while within the cities of Britain north and south, there has been a continuous flight from inner city to suburbs. This shift has also resulted in a significant 'levelling upwards' which has had continu-ing political consequences, with a steady shift since 1950 from pro-Labour working-class seats to pro-Tory middle-class ones at each parliamentary redistribution. One result of this is that the remaining areas of poverty and unemployment – of course increased greatly by the recent recession – have become much more visible and squalid, though diminishing as a proportion of Britain's total social milieu.

None of the points made here, although significant, seems centrally to address a number of matters of primary importance in affecting living standards and income distribution. The major change which has occurred amongst the whole of the British population during the past generation has been a major rise in property ownership, especially home ownership, such that a majority of all households – a majority which is continuously increasing, despite Britain's notoriously poor economic performance – are now property owners. Along with this has occurred increasing evidence of wealth and income equalization. The reason for the second of these changes is more complex – though it must clearly be related to the first. As to the first of these changes, the question which must be addressed is why the majority of the population prior to the present generation failed to become property owners. The main reason for this – and we have not yet directly examined this point – is that until the Second World War or after the majority of the working classes – some 70–80 per cent of the population – were in the main simply too poor to accumulate property. Apart from a minority of skilled labourers, working-class incomes were simply too low, and their working lives too often broken by bouts of unemployment, to make meaningful property accumulation possible for more than a minority. To this basic fact must be added all those other factors discussed, from population growth and large families to education-based class barriers.

This remained the case long after the initial phases of industrialization had passed. Charles Booth's famous survey of poverty in London in 1889 found that although 30.7 per cent of London's 4,309,000 inhabitants were living in poverty and 17.8 per cent comprised the lower-middle, middle, and upper-middle classes, 51.5 per cent were described as being in the 'comfortable middle classes' in Beatrice Webb's words 'existing in relative comfort and security' (Webb, II 295). Of this monumental study, which entailed an investigation of *every household in London*, Fabian pioneer Beatrice Webb (who helped to carry out the research) noted:

> It is true that the assertions of the Marxian Socialists, that the manual workers as a whole were in a state of chronic destitution, and the poor were steadily becoming poorer whilst the rich were becoming richer were not borne out . . . But [we] were confronted with a million men, women, and children in London alone, who were existing, at the best, on a family income of under 20s per week, and at worst, in a state of chronic want (Webb, II 295–6).

The majority of the working classes at the end of the nineteenth century were thus no longer in dire poverty of the Dickensian sort, but they were still too poor as yet to become property owners even though they lived – according to the meagre standards of the day – in 'relative comfort and security'.

To the other factors which have gone into the creation of a property-owning majority since 1945, three more must be added. One is the rise of nearly all incomes above the subsistence level. Net national income per head at 1900 prices rose sharply during the nineteenth century from £18.3 in 1855 to £44.1 in 1899; the rate of growth in the early twentieth century was slower, reaching £57.4 in 1937 (Mitchell and Deane, 367–8). Growth in *per capita* income, even after inflation, has been much more rapid in the post-war period. By a slightly different measure, that of real gross domestic product per head, there was precisely a doubling of *per capita* product between 1937 and 1973 (Butler and Sloman, 306–7). This tells us nothing about distribution, although as we have seen, income distribution has become much more even in recent decades. Evidently, however, even most low paid jobs are now above the minimal level to acquire property, although much has been written in recent years about the 'working poor'. One factor offsetting the social class differentials in income which still exist is the well-known fact that working-class males reach their maximum incomes at a much younger age than is the case among the middle classes. Although the long-term disadvantages of this for working-class males are obvious, the advantage seems to be that in a society where opportunities for home ownership and property acquisition are widespread, the opportunities for working-class males to acquire property at a younger age in some cases than their middle-class counterparts also exist, whereas many years of further education and junior employment must be undertaken by middle-class males before a reasonable level of income can be expected.

To this must be added a second major factor, that of women's employment. This is a complex matter, for one must distinguish historically between single working women, who have until recently been among the most underpaid and exploited of workers, and married women who, while until recently no less ill paid, have generally regarded their incomes as a pure addition to the typically larger income of the male breadwinner. In recent decades the phenomenon of working women as a commonplace even after marriage and, increasingly, throughout virtually the whole of adult life has greatly increased, as has the trend to relatively larger and larger women's incomes, the result of higher levels of education, civil rights and equal pay legislation, and the breaking down of prejudicial barriers against women's employment and promotion. A household with two breadwinners often doubles, or at least substantially raises income, and it is this factor, more perhaps than any other, which has allowed millions of families to become property owners and enjoy some of the fruits of affluence, despite all the trends which might seem on the face of it to work against the picture we have found – rising interest rates, property prices which increase far faster than inflation, higher marginal rates of taxation, and so on.

At least as important as this in the post-war world has been the third of these factors, the systematic extension of the 'web of credit' and of sources of finance for large-scale purchases like home mortgages and major consumer durables. For the great majority of the population, such a web of credit hardly existed before the Second World War, although the growth of 'semi-detached London' and the ambiance of London's new middle and lower-middle class northern suburbs during the inter-war period argues that its origins should be sought in what J.B. Priestley at the time termed the 'third England' – neither rural nor industrial – which became increasingly conspicuous in the 1920s and 1930s. The tremendous expansion of the 'never-never', of hire-purchase, of finance for automobile ownership and finally, of bank and building society finance for home ownership since the Second World War, has been at the heart of the rise in property ownership we have seen. This seems to have been the result of two trends intersecting: a rise in incomes generally and the growth of a finance network which actively seeks out, or at least cooperates in, the finance of substantial property purchases by the young and by working-class households which would have been entirely beyond the web of finance as it existed a generation before. Thus building society net mortgage advances rose from £1.6 billion in 1971 to £7.9 billion in 1982, with net mortgage advances from all loan sources rising from £1.9 billion to £13.9 billion in this period.[5] Most recently, the decision of the Thatcher government to put all council houses on sale to their tenants is a significant extension of this principle, although it must be emphasized that the rise in home ownership was well established long before the Housing Act 1980 gave tenants of local authorities a general right to buy their homes after three years. In less than three years 330,000 homes were purchased under this scheme, total private sales of houses owned by local authorities and new towns increasing from under 6000 in 1976 to over 220,000 in 1982 alone.[6]

One additional factor, less easy to define precisely, must also be noted as contributing to the changes of recent decades. This is the long-term trend to what might be termed 'psychological equality' among all social classes, to a broad similarity of experience, values, expectations, and lifestyles, especially among those born and socialized into post-war Britain. The effects of mass education, television and the media, and both the similarity of most households and the ubiquity of labour-saving devices have greatly eradicated the vast social differences which existed even a generation ago.

Although this trend has affected all social classes, it is the rich as much as any other group who have been most affected by it. The virtual end of servant keeping is a case in point: most middle-class households ceased employing a living in servant after World War One, most upper-class households after World War Two. Although this change was largely due to the shrinking of top incomes by increased taxation and to the rise in labour costs, it should be seen that broader social events since 1914 make it unlikely that servant keeping would ever return even if taxes declined to former levels. Labour-saving household appliances like the vacuum cleaner mean that one servant could now do the job of half a dozen. More basically, the growth of a desire for privacy means that living in servants would be singularly unwelcome intrusions even in some upper-class homes: as George Orwell once pointed out (in 'Shooting An Elephant') the trouble with keeping servants is that they rule you: one's every moment is devoted to putting on a show for their benefit to prove one's own superiority. And it is difficult to believe that anyone younger than, say, forty would voluntarily choose a life so at variance with contemporary mores. This might be shown by examining the life and career of Princess Diana. As the daughter of the eighth Earl Spencer and a close neighbour since birth of the Royal Family, Lady Diana Spencer grew up living probably as aristocratic and sheltered an existence as any girl born in Britain in 1961. Yet, as everyone knows, Diana worked as a kindergarten teacher, shared a London flat (admittedly an expensive one) with three flatmates, and drove a minicar; her values and tastes appear to be no different from those of most other young women of her generation, and these are far from 'aristocratic'. A comparison of the lifestyle and tastes of Princess Diana with those of other royal Princess-consorts of this century from Princess Alexandra through Princess Mary of Teck to the Queen Mother is a capsule summary of this evolution.

This trend has clearly been paralleled by the acquisition of middle-class or pseudo-middle-class tastes by the working class, so that, as socialist writers like Raymond Williams pointed out twenty years ago, there is little remaining in the way of a traditional working-class culture; in the face of an omnipresent media and mass market, there are few survivors. Much of real value and distinctiveness in modern British culture – for instance the cultured working-class autodidact – has unquestionably now been virtually lost, and most would characterize the violence and thuggery of much of today's youth culture as, at best, theatre and exhibitionism and, at worst, the second coming of Attila's more undisciplined hordes. But the gain in real living standards and in equality is often overlooked.

Short-term factors

In this section we shall examine a number of short-term factors which may have altered the general degree of inequality or the standard of living in Britain. By 'short-term factors' we do not necessarily mean those events which had an effect for a brief period of time – although some of these did – but those whose effects operate in the short term. For instance, trade unions have legally existed for over 150 years, but the effects of trade union activities on income distribution take place in the short term, and may well alter materially from decade to decade depending on such matters as the degree of unemployment and ideological militancy. The difference between 'short-term' and 'long-term' factors (discussed above) is not always clear; yet it may be useful to think in these terms. Four such short-term factors will be examined here – the effects of the World Wars, of taxation policy, of the trade unions, and of the modern Welfare State.

The two World Wars were among the most significant events of the century. Their importance for creating social change in Britain has frequently been argued by historians. The effects of the two World Wars on inequality patterns in Britain appear to have been broadly similar.[7] In both cases the wars brought about a perceptible degree of income equalization but less (or little) in the way of wealth equalization. However, in both cases there were considerable relative gains in the real incomes of the skilled working classes, and the imposition of markedly higher levels of income tax and estate duty. During the Second World War these reached 'confiscatory' levels and have not been reduced to pre-war levels by any subsequent right-wing government. In both World Wars, but especially in the Second, there were considerable shifts in social attitudes and especially in the spread of attitudes associated with 'psychological equality'. In both World Wars, two social classes appear to have been especially affected, the unionized skilled working class and the very rich. Just as the former made gains, the latter were seemingly hard hit, with taxation reaching record levels and a patriotic duty to pay them widely perceived. Additionally, a way of life was largely destroyed by the two wars – the traditional country house squirearchy in the first, the servant-keeping idle rich (and middle class) in the Second.* Some historians have argued that the World Wars have been the greatest instruments of social change in modern Britain, far greater than any deliberate redistribution brought about by government policies. Given the glacierlike slowness of changes to greater equality and a higher living standard *before* the present generation, it is difficult seriously to argue with this view. However, the changes which have occurred during the past twenty-five years probably dwarf those brought about by the two wars.

About the effects of taxation policy it is – surprisingly – at once

---

*This is to overlook all the other profound changes which were wholly or partly caused by the two wars, like the rise of Labour and the loss of empire.

easier and more difficult to speak: easier because the effects are seemingly clear-cut; more difficult because of the unknown results of tax evasion and the fact that similar changes in inequality might have occurred with different levels of taxation.

There can be little doubt that the historically high rates of income tax and death duty which have existed since before the First World War and, more particularly since the Second, have had a major influence on the real distribution of income and wealth in Britain, although the precise extent of their impact is extremely difficult to gauge and death duties might well take several generations to have a major effect upon a wealthy family's position.

Fairly low but perceptible rates of death duty, such as the ten per cent rate levied on millionaire estates by Lloyd George, might well have an invigorating effect upon the wealthy, by causing them to shift their assets from safe but low-yield investments to those potentially offering a higher return, in order to negate the effects of the death duties. In particular, it is quite possible that fear of such death duties caused the great landowners of Britain to sell much of their land and invest in higher yielding industrial shares before they would otherwise have done so, although the evidence suggests that transfer of assets from land to shares began before the period of high death duties among some families (for instance the dukes of Devonshire) while the really wholesale sales of land followed the First World War.

However, against 'confiscatory' rates of death duties, such as existed after the First World War and more particularly after the Second, no deliberate rearrangement of assets can have the desired result of avoiding the effects of these duties unless some investment can be found which literally doubles in value every few years. Although death duties are known as a 'voluntary tax' which most wealthy persons avoid, in fact many hundreds of wealthy persons in Britain have been 'caught' by these duties and their heirs have lost very substantial portions of what would otherwise have been an enormous legacy. To be sure, many others have escaped these consequences by deliberate estate duty avoidance, but on the face of it, it can hardly be doubted that Britain's wealth structure would have been even more unequally divided without death duties.

The effects of death duties on wealth equality, however, have taken many decades to be felt because death duties are only paid once in a generation and because so large a portion of the British population has hitherto accumulated no wealth at all. It is on this latter point more than any other that one may perhaps question the importance of death duties as a factor in generating greater wealth equality, for confiscating the wealth of the rich in itself does absolutely nothing to enrich the poor; indeed, in creating a climate antagonistic to investment and further wealth creation, it may well act against a dynamic, growing economy and hence against a rising degree of affluence for the poor. If this be true, the imposition of stringent death duties may well have precisely the opposite long-term consequences their proponents foresaw; in a later section we shall present some tentative comparative data which may be relevant to this question.

Higher rates of income tax have had a more immediate effect upon income distribution than probate duty has had upon wealth distribution, since the levying of income tax is continuous and sharply progressive upon all incomes above a minimal level; even during the nineteenth century, this tax usually affected the whole of the middle classes. Some of the effect which this tax may have had has not been evident because the official statistics of income ranges in Britain have normally considered pre-tax rather than after-tax incomes. If after-tax incomes are considered, the very high marginal rates of taxation enacted during the 1940s probably meant that there were no after-tax incomes higher than £10,000–15,000 for many years during the Second World War and immediate post-war period. Since there was little point even in nominally receiving a pre-tax income of such a size – 98 per cent of whose top share would be confiscated by the government – the number of pre-tax incomes of £10,000 or more also declined sharply between the 1930s and 1945–60. Fortunes were indeed earned during this period but these mainly represented rapid capital gains (as in property development) rather than savings from income. The real income of the 'average' middle-class wage earner also declined sharply in this period, hit twice by the twin scourges of unprecedented taxation and unprecedented inflation. For many years it appeared that the British middle classes might not survive at all, at least in the old sense, and what were in effect eulogies to its merits were written by nostalgic partisans. (See, for example, Lewis and Maude, *passim*.)

As we have seen, higher income tax for the well off was accompanied by a substantial increase in the relative real incomes of skilled labour, a general decline in primary poverty, and a lessening in middle and working-class income differences. The overall pattern was thus one of 'levelling up' and the question must necessarily be asked, was this the result of the most important working-class instrument of self-interested activism, the trade unions? The effects of trade union action on the working-class income levels are difficult to determine with accuracy, as is the case with so much else in this topic: there is no realistic way of determining what working-class incomes would have been like in Britain *without* trade unions. Nor are international comparisons very helpful: in the United States, where trade union membership is confined to a much smaller portion of workers than in Britain, incomes are higher, but this may be due to very long-term differences in labour costs (incomes have *always* been higher in America) than to trade union power; conversely, there are analogous countries like Australia where the trade unions are at least as powerful and their membership as numerous as in Britain, in which incomes are also higher, but again this may well be due to long-term cost factors (due in the Australian case to its isolation and small population) rather than trade union activity.

A number of basic points may, however, be made about the effects of trade unions on income levels. First, if trade unions were totally ineffective, no one would join them; the fact that trade union membership has expanded from 18 per cent of the labour force in 1911 to 31 per cent in 1938 and 47 per cent in 1970 argues that they have been perceived by millions of British workers as serving their interests. Secondly, those sections of the working-class labour force which have been least unionized, such as farm workers and shop assistants, have broadly made fewer income gains than those sections with strong unions; one wonders if the differential between white collar and skilled manual workers would not have narrowed so sharply had middle-class workers also been strongly unionized. Thirdly, it is difficult to see any continuing mechanism by which increasing company or corporate incomes would have resulted in higher wages for their employees (as opposed to higher profits) apart from the gains secured by trade union actions or their threat. Some historians have argued that increasing productivity would have resulted in higher wages in any case, but it is not easy to see how workers could have been assured of these gains.

Against these arguments may be put a number of other cogent points which suggest that the seeming power and influence of the trade unions is largely illusory. In the first place, there is the central paradox of trade union power and influence, namely that trade unions are likely to be most powerful during times of full employment, when they are least necessary, and least powerful during times of high unemployment, when they are most necessary. Trade union induced gains in relative working-class incomes have in fact been made in bursts rather than as steady, long-term gains – for instance during and just after the two World Wars and during the 1960s and 1970s – and mainly in periods of full employment. Nor can trade unions repeal the law of supply and demand or any other economic law – if union demands for sharp wage rises seriously endanger the profitability of a company, no trade union will normally make them. During the 1960s and 1970s, a period of rapid inflation without any peacetime precedent, 'exorbitant' wage demands were routinely made by unions, and often routinely granted by employers, who cheerfully passed the increase in costs on to the public. Perhaps this can be done only during a period of unprecedented inflation and an ingrained inflationary psychology.

On balance, however, the historical evidence suggests that trade unions have certainly played an important role in increasing real wages and, less certainly but probably, in achieving a long-term increase in wages as a share of national income. The success of the trade union movement has, however, not been general but confined most importantly to periods of relatively sharp gains for workers (for instance 1914–20) and to certain industries where highly organized unions can win gains much higher than those which 'market forces' would have brought about. This is the conclusion of several historical studies of the subject and it seems most sensible.[8]

A final point worth noting is that, despite the existence of trade unions for over 150 years, only recently have they been able to raise the bulk of working-class wages to a level sufficient to enjoy a 'middle-class' living standard and its accoutrements – home ownership, ownership of a car and consumer durables, some savings. As we have so often demonstrated, the 1960s, and still more the 1970s, must be seen as a watershed in property ownership and income distribution in Britain. Probably the unions speeded up a broader trend but the fact that they had failed to bring about similar living standards for their members before that suggests that broader economic and social forces were primarily responsible.

Along with the power of the trade unions, the other seemingly clear-cut source of gain for the poor in modern times has been the introduction of the Welfare State. For the purposes of this investigation, comparatively few of the benefits of the Welfare State are recorded in the statistics from which our knowledge of wealth and income distribution is derived. Two of the most important welfare entitlements, unemployment benefits and state pensions, are normally recorded in statistics of income distribution. But these statistics normally do not record the fact that there has been, since 1945, a minimum standard of entitlement below which no one may theoretically fall, nor can they measure the removal of permanent insecurity about the worst ravages of illness, old age, or unemployment which the Labour Government of 1945–51 (and, in a more limited way, its predecessors) brought about.

From the historical perspective, however, it is worth asking if the post-1945 Welfare State marked a singular and unprecedented development in modern Britain, or whether it was the culmination of a long process wherein the direst conditions of poverty were mitigated down the generations. It is a striking feature of poverty in post-Industrial Revolution Britain that in each succeeding generation the poor have become progressively less wretched. The Bombaylike squalor and degradation of Dickens' London and Engels' Manchester gave way to the still atrocious but less pervasive and awful poverty of Booth's and Rowntree's late nineteenth-century studies, when only a minority of the working class were below the line of abject poverty. By the inter-war period, as Alan S. Milward has noted, while

> the older statistical surveys of poverty in the manner of Booth and Rowntree show that it was all too possible for men to be in full employment before 1914 and to be dying of malnutrition through poverty . . . all statistical surveys also agree that this was becoming unusual in the 1920s, although the general demand for labour was much slacker. Nor does it seem that the inadequately employed and rewarded before 1914 are quite the same as the unemployed of the 1920s. (Milward, 37.)

The great social legislation of the 1940s thus came at a time when old-style poverty – despite the Depression – had changed its nature. Even in the affluent 1950s and 1960s it was notorious that poverty did continue, though it had now ceased to be a working-class phenomenon and was found in specific groups at the margins of society, especially the aged and one-parent families. The 1970s and 1980s saw the extension of this 'new poverty' to many of the young, to many coloured migrants, to workers in hard hit industries and in depressed regions. But poverty today is, if not invisible, at least materially different from that of even the 1930s, despite the steep rise in unemployment during the past decade. Most of all, this increased unemployment has occurred simultaneously with rapid and unprecedented gains in property ownership (especially among the skilled working classes) and a levelling trend in income and wealth distribution, and properly situating today's contradictory trends in their historical context appears surprisingly difficult and riddled with pitfalls. Will today's unemployed find jobs quickly in a new Britain based upon computers, advanced manufacturing processes, and an ever-larger service sector? Or are the 'two nations' destined to reappear with a vengeance, with a majority enjoying unprecedented affluence and a minority permanently out of work and disaffected? Will the old industrial centres of the north of Britain collapse still further in contrast to an ever-wealthier south, enriched still more by its proximity to Europe? Most of all, will the unprecedented gains of the past decades continue or will they cease? History can provide no answers to questions of what is to come.

Ownership and control in a capitalist economy

Many critiques of economic equality in contemporary Britain would be willing to admit that the levelling trends in income and wealth distribution, and those to the ever-greater ownership of property, are certainly correct, but would insist that to concentrate on these aspects alone of the question of economic equality in modern Britain is largely to miss the real heart of the matter.

Even if the working classes are far more prosperous than in the past – a contention itself highly arguable in view of today's massive unemployment and underemployment, as well as the virtual 'deindustrialization' of Britain's northern cities – this conceals the perpetuation and continuing existence of a small, self-selected, and unresponsible class of wealth holders and economic controllers who own grossly disproportionate shares of the national wealth and effectively own or control the most important business corporations and concerns in Britain, as well as much privately owned land. Nearly all of these economic controllers are drawn from the social backgrounds of the upper middle class and above, and most from among the wealthy, often inheriting vast fortunes. Most attended one of a handful of expensive public schools like Eton and Harrow, and owe their privileged positions to their inherited wealth, social backgrounds, common education and the 'old school tie' rather than to any innate talent. Many if not most also acquire and share information and business opportunities by virtue of membership in privileged organizations like London's clubs. Although 'self-made men' can on occasion become wealthy enough or powerful enough to be accepted by the economic 'Establishment', their number is small and such men almost invariably acquire the political and social outlook of those born to wealth in a short period of time. This economic Establishment is responsible to no one but itself, least of all to the workers in its companies or to users or consumers of its products. It is especially strong and well represented in the City of London, has strong and continuing links with the traditional landed aristocracy and with the higher echelons of the Conservative Party. It is less well represented in Britain's manufacturing industries and, arguably as a result, private investment from the banks and leading institutions of the City into Britain's heavy industries has for decades been withheld at the expense of investment overseas or in highly profitable, but economically and socially useless areas like property development, to Britain's long-term and severe economic detriment. Overall, the record of Britain's economic controllers since 1945 if not long before has manifestly been lamentable and the privileged, cushioned, hidebound, and feckless nature of the economic Establishment must bear a major share of the blame. Some versions of this critique would also mention Britain's nationalized industries as they have come to exist since 1945. Like the privately owned sector of the economy, their governing boards are also unrepresentative, frequently make decisions which are contrary to the national interest or the interest of consumers, and are to a surprising extent composed of men drawn from much the same social backgrounds as the economic Establishment. (For a general discussion of this viewpoint, see for example Scott and the readings in Urry and Wakeford.)

Abundant evidence can seemingly be produced to support the thesis outlined here. Certainly really vast fortunes do exist in contemporary Britain. The Duke of Westminster, owner of the ground rents of Oxford Street, Mayfair and Pimlico, is frequently said to be worth at least £2 billion. Before his death in 1973, 2nd Bt Sir John Ellerman's fortune was often estimated at £500 million, as was the wealth of such London property developers as Harry Hyams and Lord Samuel of Wych Cross during the property boom of the early 1970s. Certainly there exist at least several thousand millionaires in Britain today, and several hundred at least worth £5 million or more.

Not all significant company chairmen own the assets of their companies. Increasingly, as is well known, company chairmen and other extremely influential directors of large companies are managers promoted for their abilities who often own virtually no assets in these companies, earning essentially only their salaries. Occasionally, as with Donald Stokes (later Lord Stokes), chairman of British Leyland, such managers begin life in meagre circumstances and actually rise from the shop floor, but such true life rags-to-riches stories are still extremely rare and almost never occur in any prestigious City of London firms. Overwhelmingly, however, at least a superficial analysis of the social and educational backgrounds of major company chairmen and other economic controllers reveals the near impossibility of anyone, regardless of his talent, from below the upper middle class at least rising to economic leadership. One important study of 460 major British company chairmen between 1900 and 1970 found that only 1 per cent emerged from working-class backgrounds, 10 per cent from the middle class and no less than 66 per cent from what the researchers termed the 'upper class' (Stanworth and Giddens, 83).[9] This study found surprisingly little evidence of any widening of social opportunities for promotion to company chairmen, at least up to 1970. According to perhaps the most commonly employed measure of the social origins of 'elite' groups, attendance at a major public school, while 75 per cent of those company chairmen born in 1820–39 attended no public school, 74 per cent of those born in 1900–19 did so. The percentage attending Eton or Harrow, the most prestigious schools, actually increased from 22 to 31 per cent.[10] (*Ibid.*, 90.) Equally clearly there would also appear to be a number of discernible and traceable 'commonalities' among Britain's top business leaders. At least 46 per cent of the directors of large financial institutions in the City of

London were members of one or more among nine prestigious London clubs (Brooks's, Boodle's, etc.) according to one study, as were 28 per cent of 261 directors of leading industrial concerns around 1970 (Whitley in Stanworth and Giddens, 70). Some researchers have carefully analysed the networks of overlapping directorships, especially between the banks and industrial companies (Whitley in Stanworth and Giddens, 74; Aaronovitch; Lipton and Wilson *passim*; Scott and Hughes *passim*).

Given these 'commonalities' it is not surprising that key decisions in contemporary British economic life have been made by men drawn from the same exclusive backgrounds – not uncommonly, actually relatives of one another, and often linked as well to Britain's largest financial, commercial, and industrial concerns. Although the personnel and events are now nearly thirty years old, perhaps the 1957 Bank Rate Tribunal, a Parliamentary investigation into power and decision making at the Bank of England (which at the time had been nationalized for eleven years!) brought these linkages out more clearly than any other investigation in the post-war years. At the time, according to the Marxist sociologist Sam Aaronovitch, the Committee of Treasury of the Bank of England were composed of:

C.F. Cobbold, Governor, related to the Hambro family of whom Sir Charles Hambro is a Director of the Bank; H.C.B. Mynors, Deputy-Governor (whose brother was temporary Principal HM Treasury in 1940, and who is related to the Brand family – of Lazards – and more distantly, to the Colvilles of Rothschilds); Sir G.L. Bolton, Executive Director at the time, who since then has become Chairman of the Bank of London and South America, and a director of consolidated Zinc Corporation, Sun Life Assurance Company of Canada and other concerns; G.C. Eley, Chairman of British Drug Houses, British Bank of the Middle East, chairman of Richard Crittal, director of Equity and Law Life Assurance Company and others; Sir John Hanbury Williams, chairman of Courtaulds – into which family married Hon. R.A. Butler; Basil Sanderson, chairman of Shaw, Saville and Albion Company and of Aberdeen and Commonwealth Line, director of Ford Motor Company, Furness Withy, Dalgety and Company, etc., and Minister of War Transport, 1941–5; and finally, Lord Bicester, head of Morgan Grenfell, director of Shell, Vickers, etc. (Aaronovitch in Urry and Wakeford, 125).[11]

More generally, the ownership or control of substantial amounts of

capital such as the companies and firms noted here, or the ownership of very substantial amounts of private wealth, it is often
argued by proponents of the same critique, confer upon their
holders the power of significant decision making in the guidance of
broader events (Parkin *passim*). This power is only rarely exercised
in an explicit way for the power of capital

> . . . is revealed much less in positive acts of decision making . . .
> than in the everyday, for much of the time unquestioned, application
> of those assumptions which give priority to private capital accumu-
> lation . . . Power is to be found more in uneventful routine than in
> conscious and active exercise of will. (Thomas citing Westergaard and
> Resler, *The Wealth Report*, 145.)

The viewpoint examined so far in this section is often associated
with a Marxist or left-wing Labour critique of British capitalism.
Many Marxist sociologists would argue that the privilege and
power of a small elite are necessary and inevitable adjuncts of
advanced capitalism, the British situation mirroring that in all other
developed capitalist societies. Britain may well differ from other
such societies in the unusual degree of separation of its financial
oligarchy in the City of London from Britain's industrial base in
the north, with the long-term weakness of its manufacturing
sector, but in most other respects it is similar to other Western
societies.

Those whose ideological presuppositions are not of the left
would, naturally, disagree with much of this critique. It is undeniable, however, that most leading British chairmen, especially in
finance, were and are drawn from backgrounds of wealth and
privilege, although the mere attendance of such persons at a public
school certainly does not in itself prove that the origins and
backgrounds of these persons were wealthy; to establish this,
research must provide independent evidence about their actual
family status and wealth, and detailed evidence about this often
shows much less privilege than one might imagine (Rubinstein,
'Education'). The situation, moreover, appears to be becoming
more open to the rise of men from non-elite backgrounds, albeit
slowly and less decisively in finance than in industry. However,
both of the Governors of the Bank of England during the 1970s, Sir
Leslie O'Brien and Gordon Richardson, came from distinctly non-
elite educational backgrounds – their secondary schooling was,

respectively, at Wandsworth School and Nottingham High School – and were neither wealthy nor related to any wealthy or powerful families.

Nor does this critique offer sufficient prominence to the well-known distinctions among business leaders and company chairmen into the self-made tycoons who substantially owned the assets of their companies, the asset-owning business leaders who inherited their means – usually the sons or grandsons of the founder or chief builder of a firm – and managers who own little or nothing of the firms they manage.

Self-made asset-owning tycoons have appeared throughout modern British history, often in 'fringe' areas, or in newer developing areas of the economy. For instance, what is today British Leyland was substantially founded by William Morris, later Lord Nuffield, who began life as a garage mechanic and rose to be one of the half-dozen richest men in Britain. ICI was founded in the nineteenth century by chemical makers of immigrant stock, John Brunner from Switzerland, and Ludwig Mond, a German Jew, and many other leading British firms were also founded by migrants. Nearly all of the British merchant banks were also founded by migrant families, while many of the families who founded the components of the 'Big Four' clearing banks, like the Barclays and Lloyds, were Protestant dissenters originally outside and excluded from the Establishment. British business history, it is sometimes argued, has been a continuing process of outsiders becoming insiders, with one generation's new men and self-made dynasties becoming part of the Establishment several generations later. There is no evidence that this process has stopped; indeed, the post-war period may have seen a quickening of the pace of upward mobility by self-made men.

Admittedly, most of today's business leaders are not self-made men, but the descendants of former self-made tycoons or business managers not themselves owning their company's assets. The succession of the descendants of yesterday's tycoons inevitably raises the problem of their competence. It is often argued that the descendants of yesterday's 'players' are today's 'gentlemen', incompetent dynamically to manage a business concern (Coleman *passim*); if that is indeed so, their incompetence merely leaves the way open for new men of greater abilities. Similarly, although the managerial chairmen of business concerns may come from middle-class backgrounds (or above), if they are not competent business-men, their company profits will quickly diminish. Whatever the social backgrounds of leading businessmen, they are subject to precisely the same business pressures and market strategies; if the next chairman of ICI were a promoted janitor, he would still have to react to precisely the same business circumstances as if he was an old Etonian, and if some companies fail to promote able and competent executives regardless of background, others which do promote them will simply perform better – or so common sense tells us.

More basically, those who dispute the accuracy of this critique frequently argue that it concentrates upon economic power at the expense of other types of influence in society (Dahrendorf *passim*). Britain's most important businesses and business leaders are plainly powerful institutions and men in contemporary society, but so are others including the state, trade unions, professional bodies, the media and so on. Trade unions, the Labour Party and many of the instrumentalities of the state like the welfare network arose in this century specifically as a 'countervailing force' – to use Galbraith's term describing the post-New Deal American economy (Galbraith *passim*) – to the inequalities allegedly created by capitalism and their key personnel have generally been drawn from among the working classes. It is likely that the man in the street would find it difficult to believe that Labour cabinets and the trade unions were not fully as powerful (in whatever sense this is meant) as Britain's major corporations and wealthy men. One might illustrate this in human terms with a historical comparison: during the 1945–51 Labour period the Duke of Westminster, Sir John Ellerman, and Lord Catto (then Governor of the Bank of England) were among the wealthiest men, and most prominent capitalists, in the country. But is it really credible that they were more powerful than the former dockworker Ernest Bevin, the former Welsh coal miner Aneurin Bevan, or the Cockney ex-policeman Herbert Morrison, all at the time key ministers in the Attlee cabinet?

A number of other basic points are often raised against the depiction of a capitalist elite outlined above. Although Britain's leading businessmen may be seen as a small, powerful, wilful, cooperative (indeed, conspiring) group, as businessmen they are also rivals whose economic interests may well be widely divergent, indeed antagonistic. Similarly, while the economic elite may be depicted as closely cooperating with the government and the state apparatus, the interests of the government and the party in power, above all in securing reelection, may differ widely and basically from those of the business elite and major business units; when Labour is in power, left-wing backbench pressure, and Labour's trade union and working-class constituency, will invariably make any such relationship much more difficult.

Critics of this viewpoint also point out that under any economic or social system, key decision makers will almost certainly, and virtually by definition, be small in number and enjoy pay and privileges substantially above those of the average man. In the Soviet Union and its satellites, key economic decisions are also taken by a small, privileged elite. While it is true that under a Marxist regime there is no ownership of the shares of major business corporations or institutions, the regime is also thoroughly totalitarian in most other respects, especially in the realm of civil liberties, and there seems throughout this century clearly to be an association between capitalism and freedom of thought, belief and expression, and between statist regimes of the far right and left and totalitarianism.

Further, increasingly the ownership of shares in the major British corporations is no longer in the hands of individual tycoons or their families, but consists of ownership by pension funds, insurance companies, and even trade unions. At the present time the largest pension funds are those of the nationalized industries. In 1983, the assets of the pension funds of the eight largest nationalized industries (the Post Office, National Coal Board, British Railways, etc.) amounted to £16,062 million, invested in private shares and government securities (Sampson, 324). Nationalized industries are thus among the very largest owners of 'private enterprise' in Britain. Even the very wealthiest private capitalists in Britain must now individually be dwarfed by what *The Economist* has termed the 'private corporate state'.

Finally, although the historical development of capitalism in Britain may indeed be unique in some respects, especially in the separation of the City, the financial heart, and industry, there are other contemporary societies which have been more economically successful and dynamic than Britain, by the usual measurements of success, while comprising an economic elite both wealthier and more castelike than Britain's. In America, the very wealthiest multi-millionaires have for over a century been far richer than their British colleagues. No one in Britain remotely approached the wealth of a Rockefeller or Ford at the turn of the century (Rubinstein, 1981, 247–8). Historically, Britain was extremely late in developing a sector of corporate grants, and the most striking feature of the British industrial economy in the nineteenth century was its dominance by relatively small-scale or medium-sized firms, nearly all family owned and controlled. Britain produced no one like J.P. Morgan, the great banker who allegedly 'controlled' much of America's economy at the turn of the century (Rubinstein, 1981, 247–8; Payne; Gatrell). In 1984, *Forbes* magazine listed twelve Americans as worth $1 billion (about £800 million) or more; certainly they were far more numerous than their British equivalents. The size and economic influence of America's leading corporations also dwarf Britain's. In Japan, perhaps the most dynamic economy of all, the closed, castelike nature of business leadership and of the leading business families is widely celebrated, as is the virtually neo-feudal attitude of lifetime dedication to the company expected of all employees. In France, whose economy has also grown significantly faster than Britain's since the war, the nexus between the state and private industry via its elite tertiary institutions like the Ecole Nationale d'Administration is much stronger than in Britain. Compared with nearly every other country with an impressive economic record in the contemporary period, Britain's economic elite appears unusually weak in one or another crucial respect, and it is this weakness, rather than its purported strength, which may be at the heart of what most observers have seen as Britain's wretched economic performance over the past forty years.

Social mobility and economic opportunity

Closely related to the contention that a small and powerful economic elite exists in Britain is the issue of social mobility and the realistic opportunities for rising by one's abilities and talents, regardless of wealth or family background, into a 'higher' social class and status. So long as substantial amounts of property are normally inherited by the close heirs of the propertied minority and especially the very wealthy, it is often suggested this must act to perpetuate inequality across the generations. Similarly, so long as higher education and 'elite' secondary education is largely the domain of the middle and upper classes and above, and so long as there is a nexus between such education and well-paying employment, inequality is also perpetuated. At the very highest levels of society, it is often contended, realistic opportunities for promotion or success have existed only for those drawn from wealthy families or 'elite' educational backgrounds in the great majority of cases. But even if everything said about these factors by their critics is correct – and the amount of confusion and exaggeration attending, for example, the connection between parents' affluence, public school education, and life chances is very considerable – these factors can, at their worst, only reproduce the inequalities of the past generation in the next. Since measurable inequality has been declining in a marked fashion during the past generation, at a rate probably far outstripping the small proportion of the population educated at a fee-paying school or inheriting substantial means, it can be argued that other factors at work in Britain's economic and social order are more significant than these institutions (or others) which perpetuate inequality.

This important point is often overlooked by commentators on Britain's continuing social inequalities. It may be argued that Britain's elites possessed a vested interest in perpetuating themselves and their status in the past, but whose interest is served by the vast expansion of educational opportunities and of property ownership since 1945? The answer must be, paradoxically, both the elites and the non-elites; the elites for removing the cause of the most perceived and perceptible relative deprivation which might challenge their reign, the non-elites for the concomitant gains in wealth and status.

On the matter of social mobility and inheritance, a good deal of research has been undertaken by sociologists and economists. Among the very rich, there is little doubt that the percentage of 'self-made men' – those who literally go from rags to riches – has always been low, although their number is not and has never been nonexistent. Investigating the social origins of wealthy British males deceased in 1924–6 (from the probate records), Josiah Wedgwood found that 57 per cent of men leaving £200,000 or more were the sons of fathers who themselves left £50,000 or more with 67 per cent the sons of men leaving £10,000 or more. On the other hand, 18 per cent of such persons were the sons of fathers leaving less than £1000 (Wedgwood, 155–83).

The contemporary economist C.D. Harbury investigated in detail the economic origins of a sample of men leaving £100,000 or more in Britain in 1956–7 and 1965, and found that 52 per cent of the former group and 45 per cent of the latter were the sons of fathers who themselves left £100,000 (in constant terms) or more, while respectively 76 per cent and 77 per cent were the sons of fathers who left £10,000 (constant terms) (Harbury and MacMahon, Table II; see also Harbury *passim*). This means, of course, that 24 per cent and 23 per cent were the sons of fathers who left less than £10,000, and many of these were 'self-made men'. Even among millionaires deceased in Britain since the early nineteenth century a low but not negligible portion began life poor or in relatively meagre circumstances and increased their economic rewards literally by hundreds of thousands of times. One of the classic examples was probably Sir John Ellerman (1862–1933), father of the shipping magnate already mentioned (p. 136), probably Britain's richest-ever businessman in real terms, whose father was an immigrant corn factor in Hull who left £600; Ellerman left an incredible £37 million at the bottom of the Great Depression. Somewhere between 4.8 and 24.8 per cent of Britain's business millionaires of the 1808–1939 period began life poor, depending on how rigorously this is defined (Rubinstein, *Men of Property*, 125–6). The great majority of million-aires were the sons of fairly affluent businessmen, although only a minority were themselves born rich (*Ibid.*, 122–5). Lord Leverhulme (1851–1926), the millionaire soap king whose father was a moderately successful local soap manufacturer who left £70,000, is fairly typical of the progress of Britain's best known tycoons. Of course starting rich – or with at least some capital, business connections, or business expertise – is helpful to future success, but it is not necessary and opportunities have always existed for the particularly lucky or enterprising to rise into the economic elite without any of these supports. Apparently the 'self-made man' is becoming more common in Britain not less (*Ibid.*, 240–1).

Among the entire population, several large scale studies of intergenerational social mobility in modern Britain have been undertaken, linking the occupation of fathers and sons. The two best known were undertaken by D.V. Glass in 1949 and J.H. Goldthorpe *et al* (known as the Oxford Social Mobility Group) in 1972. Both studies showed – as one might expect – that being the son of a father in a higher socio-economic class increased one's own chances of achieving similar status very markedly; conversely, the sons of the poor tended to stay poor. In the 1949 study, the so-called 'Index of Association' or 'mobility index' for Class I fathers and sons was 13:1, indicating that thirteen times as many sons of social Class I fathers themselves obtained Class I jobs as would be expected on a random basis (Heath, 62). By 1972, however, this ratio had diminished to 4:1, and the 1972 study probably found a loosening up of real opportunities for social mobility, in the overall context of general class stability between generations and of a relative rise (as has been discussed above) in white collar, middle-class employment (*Ibid.*, 62–4). In 1972, 23.6 per cent of social Class I respondents in the Oxford survey were the sons of social Class I fathers, but 29.0 per cent were sons of working-class (social Class VI and VII on this scale) fathers (*Ibid.*, 63). Given the significant class-linked basis of education and inheritance, as well as relative discrimination against those from some British regions, minority ethnic groups, and women (not surveyed in these studies), it would be naive to expect anything more than an historical improvement over the decades in such statistics. But, equally, it would be naive to expect anything more than a historical increasing educational opportunities and an increase in the number of middle-class positions. It is also arguable whether ability and talent is or is not randomly distributed; these, too, may be class linked to a measurable degree. Finally, some sociologists have argued that rates of intergenerational social mobility may be quite similar in nearly all modern societies, and related more to the functional structure of management positions among industrial societies than to other factors like inherited wealth or the education system (Bendix and Lipset, 13).

Summary: Economic equality and inequality

The discussion in this section seems to have confirmed the view stated briefly in an earlier chapter, that trends in economic equality in contemporary Britain are both more difficult to determine with consensus or accuracy than is the case with legal, political, or social equality, and seem to demonstrate patterns which pull, as it were, in several directions at once. Broad trends in wealth and income distribution, and gains in living standards and property ownership, seem to indicate growing and, in some respects, unprecedented degrees of equality (with bastions of privilege remaining) while those who perceived the existence of a class-based economic elite see little or no evidence of its passing. Opportunities for inter-generational social mobility appear to be broadening, but a middle-class (or higher) origin still goes far to ensure later success, while a working-class background is unquestionably a great handicap to anyone's life chances.

More fundamentally, there is no consensus on whether there *ought* to be equality or near equality in the economic sphere. Nearly everyone would admit that enterprise and talent ought to be well rewarded, most questions of equity in this area revolve around the tolerable limits of inequality and the status of inherited wealth or institutions, like the public schools, which seem to many to per-petuate inequality across the generations. On the political right in Britain, there are many who now argue that in Sir Keith Joseph's words, Britain needs 'more inequality' and that the levelling pat-terns in inequality and distribution which occurred during and after the Second World War went too far to penalizing enterprise, thrift, and talent. At the other extreme, an increasingly important stream within the Labour Party sees the persisting degrees of wealth and income inequality as deplorable, and puts a thoroughgoing attack on economic inequality close to the forefront of its agenda. It is clear that this debate is a very live one indeed in contemporary Britain, and, unlike the arguments which have surrounded other facets of equality, is unlikely to be resolved by consensus in our time.

IV

Economic equality:
Britain and the world –
some comparisons

In this final chapter we will consider some relevant international comparisons in order to place the British experience in its proper perspective. Throughout this work, the lack of accurate historical statistics, and the difficulties which lie in the way of fully accepting those which do exist, have repeatedly been stressed, and these factors apply *a fortiori* to comparisons with other nations. Even the most basic economic facts – never mind those which are rather esoteric – are often measured in slightly different ways elsewhere, while the historical statistics of economic development are seldom as good as those for Britain, inadequate as these may seem to us.

Perhaps the most relevant national comparison is with the United States. Historical statistics on the share of national wealth owned by the top one per cent of wealth owners have been compiled for the period 1922–1972 by a number of American economic historians, especially Robert J. Lampman and James D. Smith. According to their research, the wealth ownership among the richest 1 per cent has evolved in this manner:

TABLE 17: Percentage share of American personal wealth owned by the top 1 per cent of wealth owners, 1922–72

	Per cent		Per cent		Per cent
1922	31.6	1949	20.8	1972	20.7
1929	36.3	1954	24.0		
1933	28.3	1956	23.8		
1939	30.6	1958	23.4		
1945	23.3	1969	20.1		

Source: *Statistical Abstract of the United States, 1982–83* (Washington, DC, 1982), p. 449.

It will be seen that wealth holding became markedly more

concentrated during the 'roaring twenties', declined very considerably in concentration as a result of the Depression, and never thereafter rose to its pre-1929 levels. Concentration again declined very markedly during the Second World War, rose again during the 1950s, and has declined slightly since. (Apparently no data more recent than 1972 is available, but information on income distribution and home ownership will be considered shortly which suggests, at least tentatively, that wealth distribution has probably not altered significantly since 1972.)

Although there has been a broadly continuing decline in the share of American wealth owned by the rich, changes in the distribution of wealth appear to be much more closely and immediately correlated with major economic and political events like the Depression and the Second World War than has been the case in Britain. Possibly this is because American wealth is held disproportionately in the form of shares traded on a particularly volatile share market rather than (as in Britain) in the form of land, house properties, and relatively stable government securities. How does the evolution of wealth holding by the rich in America compare with that in Britain? Table 17 (p. 147) reveals some striking differences. Wealth distribution among Britain's top 1 per cent was markedly less equal during the earlier part of this century, but has evolved toward greater equality in a much more consistent and striking way than in America. The decline in the dominant position of the rich in Britain has, moreover, been steady and relatively less affected by larger events like the Second World War than is the case in America. Although there is no American data more recent than 1972, the picture for Britain (Tables 9 and 10) is one of a continuing trend to greater equality, such that the richest 1 per cent of the population in Britain owned at most only marginally more in 1981 – and on some measurements rather less – than did the richest 1 per cent of Americans in 1972.

Turning to income distribution in the United States, the historical data is less extensive and not comparable to the distribution shown in Table 17. However, something of the evolution of trends in American family incomes in constant dollars from 1960 to 1981 may be seen in Table 18.

For what it is worth in terms of a comparison with the British statistics, this American data shows a distinct 'levelling up' up to 1975, but much less in the way of improving statistics

TABLE 18: Money income of American families, percentage distribution by income level in constant (1981) dollars

				Percentage distribution of families, by income level				
Date	Under 5000	5000– 9999	10,000– 14,999	15,000– 19,999	20,000– 24,999	25,000– 34,999	35,000– 49,999	50,000+	*Median Income (Dollars)*
1960	10.0	14.3	16.5	23.1	11.5	–	24.7	–	17,259
1965	7.2	12.5	14.0	20.7	11.5	–	34.1	–	20,054
1970	5.1	10.3	12.1	17.6	10.7	25.5	11.2	7.5	23,111
1975	4.5	11.4	12.7	12.9	13.2	25.7	11.5	8.0	23,183
1981	5.8	11.5	13.6	12.6	12.6	20.2	14.9	8.9	22,388

Source: *Statistical Abstract of the United States, 1982–83*, 432

thereafter. Indeed, the median American income actually declined between 1975 and 1981 in real terms, doubtless because of the recession of the late 1970s and also, in all likelihood, because of the rising numbers of one-parent families and the aged. It was recently reported that in 1982 the top 2 per cent of income earners received about 15 per cent of all income, suggesting a somewhat greater level of income inequality than in Britain. However, the top 10 per cent of all American income earners received 33 per cent of all income in 1982 compared with 29 per cent in 1969, suggesting that a slight deterioration in the distribution of American incomes has occurred since the 1960s (*The Australian* (Sydney) 5 October 1984).

The evolution of housing tenure in the United States can be traced for a much longer period and in much greater precision. This is done in Table 19, which compares owner-occupied and renter-occupied housing units from 1920 to 1980.

The pattern here resembles that found for American wealth ownership discussed above. Prior to the 1960s, the American statistics are incomparably better than the British, with twice or nearly twice the rate of owner occupation in America as in Britain down to the 1950s. The early advantage of the United States was not merely a general function of the greater median income levels in the United States – although this was a major factor in the difference – but of the very high rates of owner occupation in the comparatively large farm sector of the United States. In 1920 58.1 per cent of occupied housing units on farms (farm residency still amounted to 35.3 per cent of all American households) were owner occupied; in 1930 and

TABLE 19: Occupied American housing units, by tenure and percentage, 1920–80

Year	Percentage of occupied units	
	Owner occupied	*Renter occupied*
1920	45.6	54.4
1930	47.8	52.2
1940	43.6	56.4
1950	55.0	45.0
1960	61.9	38.1
1970	62.9	37.1
1976	64.7	35.3
1978	65.2	34.8
1980	65.6	34.4

Source: *Statistical Abstract of the United States, 1982–83*, 762

1940 – despite the Depression – farm owner occupancy was still 53.9 and 53.2 per cent of the total.

From the 1960s onwards, however, the American levels of owner occupancy hardly rose at all; in particular, the rise during the recession-ridden later 1970s was almost nonexistent. In contrast, the British statistics show a steady gain. Although the British levels of owner occupancy, now about 60 per cent, are still somewhat lower than the American levels, the gap is apparently narrowing steadily and may well be entirely accounted for by the two factors of a relatively higher percentage of elderly persons in Britain and the much lower rates of owner occupancy found in Britain outside of England, in part a result of local historical and political trends. On an age-specific basis, it may be that owner-occupancy rates are virtually identical in the two countries at present for most younger age groups.

There is also some data for Australia, although it is probably less reliable than for Britain. In 1915, according to Australia's War Census of Income and Wealth, the top 1 per cent of adults in Australia owned 37.8 per cent of all wealth, the top 1 per cent of all males, 39.3 per cent of wealth owned by all males. For the top 10 per cent these percentages were both 78.1 per cent. For the period 1967–72 a number of contemporary economists had estimated that the top 1 per cent of Australian individual wealth holders owned between 22.0 and 28.7 per cent of all private wealth, the top 10 per cent between 58.5 and 72.7 per cent.[1] The pattern here is much closer to that in the United States than to Britain, and this resemblance is also apparently paralleled by levels of owner occupancy, which rose from about 40 per cent (in Sydney) during the 1930s to a national level of 66.7 per cent in 1976. No comparable data on Australian wealth distribution exists for the very recent period, but it was widely reported in the Australian media during the late 1970s and early 1980s that levels of owner occupancy were no longer rising and may have been declining slightly. If one may infer from this that the Australian picture continues to resemble the American in showing a slowing down in the previously steady gains in rising living standards, this must again – however tentatively – be contrasted with the picture of Britain.

Perhaps little can truly be inferred about Britain from an international comparison of this sort. Nevertheless, the findings here are consistent with much of what we have found in this discussion of economic equality in Britain – a marked improvement, against all expectations, so that in relative terms Britain appears to have caught up with those comparable countries which long boasted a higher standard of living. From this conclusion, of course, very little can be said about economic equality as such, but the evidence would appear to be inconsistent with the view that economic conditions in Britain are worsening or even with the view that they have remained largely unchanged.

Notes

I. Introduction

1 Some recent works on twentieth-century British history may, however, be seen as part of the 'elitist' framework. These include works emphasizing the 'corporatist' elements in British political history in which the most significant interest groups, especially big business, the trade unions, and the state are seen as combining to determine the direction of policy, and the so-called 'high politics' histories of the incorporation of Labour into the political mainstream. An example of the former is Middlemas; of the latter, Cowling.

2 To this day, the nature of some major institutions in Britain like its head of state, the monarch, and most of the House of Lords, is decided by the 'pre-modern' criterion of heredity.

3 Prior to the nineteenth century, Roman Catholics, especially in Ireland, suffered from far more legal restrictions than other non-Anglican religious groups and were the subject of considerable elite and popular hostility. For instance, from 1700 to 1778 Catholics could not buy or inherit land in Britain, while Catholics could not vote in Ireland from 1727 to 1793, despite comprising the great majority of the population.

4 It should not be forgotten that election campaigns in Britain were often rowdy and even violent affairs prior to the First World War.

5 By which they meant universal manhood suffrage; the idea of giving the vote to all adult women would have struck all observers at the time as preposterous.

6 Moreover until the First World War General Elections were held over a period of two to three weeks rather than on a single day, enabling persons with several votes to travel from constituency to constituency to vote.

7 Many political scientists believe that it is inflated by the so-called 'law

of cubes' – the total number of MPs elected by each party to Parliament equals its percentage of the *cube* of all votes cast for all parties. This greatly magnifies the proportion of all seats won by the largest party.

II.   The Historical development of income and wealth distribution in Britain

1   There have been rudimentary death duties on personal property in Britain since 1694. Both personal and real (i.e. landed) wealth passing at death have been taxed since 1894.

2   For an excellent analysis of the deficiencies of the probate data as a means of calculating inequality, see Polanyi and Wood, 23–44.

3   For a list of all very large estates (£3 million or more to 1969, then £5 million or more) left between 1940 and 1979, see Rubinstein, *Men of Property*, 228–9. At least 105 estates worth £1 million or more were left in Britain between September 1983 and August 1984, despite the recession and the vested interest these wealthy persons seemingly had in estate duty avoidance.

4   For those who were interested in my *Men of Property* list, and for the sake of completeness, these recent large estates were left by: Sir Charles Clore, financier, £28.3 million; Henry J.R. Bankes, Dorset landowner, £21.6 million; Gerald, 6th Earl of Bradford, landowner, £18.3 million; Sir Maxwell Joseph, hotels and entertainment, £17.3 million; Alfred C. Beatty, mining fortune, £12.5 million; David, 6th Marquess of Exeter, landowner, £8.8 million; Mrs Gladys D. Sprinks, £7.8 million; Charles, 7th Baron Sherborne, landowner, £7.0 million; Peter Whitbread, land and breweries, £6.8 million; Mrs Elsie F. Hunnisett, £6.4 million; Dr Colin A. McDonnell of Dublin, £6.1 million; Mrs Barbara Green (sister of West End impresario Larry Parkes), £5.6 million; Eileen Walton, supermarket heiress, £5.5 million; Miss Catherine Godman, Scottish landowner, £5.0 million; finally, Kenneth, Baron Clark of Saltwood, the celebrated art historian, left £5.3 million. Lord Clark was the scion of a millionaire nineteenth-century cotton dynasty and had built up a valuable personal art collection. It is obvious that the phenomenal rise in land values since about 1960 has been the major cause of many of these fortunes, while the fact that agricultural land is taxed at a considerably lower rate than other assets makes it more advantageous to own.

5   This table is derived from A.J. Harrison, 'Trends Over Time in the Distribution of Wealth', in Jones ed., *Economics and Equality*.

6   Printed in *American Economic Review* 45 (March 1955).

7   *Economic History Review*, 2nd ser., 21 (1968).

8   Those interested in studying King's 1688 returns in more detail should consult Deane, 7–11; Deane and Cole, 155–8; and Holmes, *passim*.

9   Soltow's essay does not mention Joseph Massie's social tables for 1759, which are somewhat similar to King's and Colquhoun's in format. Massie (who was writing to attack the West Indian sugar interest) included fifty-one socio-economic classes in his analysis, grouped under four most extraordinary headings: 'labouring families, etc.', 'families which drink Tea or Coffee occasionally', 'families which drink Tea or Coffee in the Morning' and 'families which drink Tea, Coffee, or Chocolate, Morning and Afternoon' (!) On Massie's work, see Mathias, *passim*.

10 Deane and Cole, 325; Mitchell and Deane, 430. Deane and Cole note that 'The conclusion that Schedule D assessments were undervalued is strongly supported by examination of the figures' (p. 327) but provide no really compelling explanation for this view.

11 The 'landed' portion includes incomes assessed under Schedules A and B, together with one-half of Schedule C. Schedule B was levied upon only a portion of farmers' total incomes, ranging from one-third to three-quarters. The Schedule B figures have thus been revised upward to take this omitted portion into account.

    The 'business/professional' portion includes incomes assessed under Schedules D and E, and one-half of Schedule C. Schedule C was the tax on government securities (consols) and these were likely to be owned by the majority of propertied persons. Dividing Schedule C in half probably overstates the total 'landed' income in the earlier periods and understates it in the later decades, as newly-rich businessmen would probably have acquired an increasing proportion of government securities *vis-à-vis* landowners (there is, of course, no evidence on this point).

12 Stamp, 218–19 gives revised figures calculated as if the cutoff point for liability to the tax had been £150 throughout. Stamp does not, however, give similar figures for Schedule A, and changes in the exemption limit are not adjusted for here (from 1851 to 1876) the lower limit for exemption was £100. This will slightly raise the 'landed' proportion in 1860–1 and 1870–1 in Table 4.

13 The information in this paragraph represents a summary of Sean Glynn and John Oxborrow, 33–41. See also John Stevenson's valuable social history, 103–44 and *passim*.

14. On post-1945 poverty see Abel-Smith and Townsend, *passim* and Wedderburn, *passim*.

15 From *Social Trends* No. 13 (1983 Edition) (London, 1983), 76.

16 *Ibid.*, 87.

17 Office of Population Censuses and Surveys and General Register Office (Scotland) Statistics, cited in *Social Trends*, 114.

18 *Ibid.*, 114–15.

19 Sources: Butler and Sloman, 272 and *Social Trends*, 115. 'Local authorities' include New Towns. 'Other' includes dwellings rented with farm and business premises, or occupied by virtue of employment. It should be noted that some recent researchers believe that the percentage of pre-1914 households which were owner-occupied was substantially higher than the 10 per cent noted here, possibly around the 20 per cent mark (Swenarton and Taylor, 3).

20 See *The Twenty-Second Annual Report of the Registrar-General of Birth, Marriages, and Deaths* (1861) in the Parliamentary Papers and W.D. Rubinstein, *Men of Property*, 28–30.

21 Atkinson and Harrison, 159. See also Harrison's summary of the findings, Jones, 66–86.

22 See Daniels and Campion, *passim*; Langley, *passim*, and the *Report of the Royal Commission on the Distribution of Income and Wealth* (1976–9).

23 From *Social Trends* (1983), 78, and *Social Trends* (1984), 84. The 'top 1 per cent' etc., refers to the total United Kingdom population aged 18 or older. Estimates of the poorer sections of the population vary with differing assumptions made by the Inland Revenue. Some details on the Inland Revenue's procedures may be found in Dunn and Hoffman, *passim*.

24 However, Polanyi and Wood, 39, citing A.B. Atkinson, believe that in 1963–7, the top 1 per cent of wealth holders, adjusting for wealth 'missing' from the probate valuations and for state pensions, owned 22 per cent of all wealth, the top 5 per cent, 41 per cent of all wealth, and the top 10 per cent, 52 per cent. These figures are at some variance with those in Table 10.

25 *Social Trends* (1983), 115. This table excludes households headed by members of the armed forces, full-time students, and those who have never worked.

26 *Ibid.*, 87.

27 *Ibid.*, 88.

28 *Ibid.*, 182. 'Other non-Europeans' included household heads of Arab, Chinese, not stated, and mixed origin.

29 Obviously, low levels of property ownership are a result of pre-existing poverty rather than the reverse, but the differential in statistics for Asian as opposed to West Indian households suggests very different pathways of opportunity and group behaviour.

30 *Social Trends* (1984), 93.

III. *The pattern of income and wealth inequality in Britain: interpretation*

1 For a scholarly study of this subject dating from 1920, see T.H.C. Stevenson, *passim*.

2 Earlier figures exist from the 1811 and 1821 censuses concerning the number of British *families* employed in 'agricultural occupations'. These percentages were (1811) 35.2 per cent and (1821) 33.3 per cent.

3 Namely transport and communications, mining, metal and machinery manufacturing, chemicals, textiles, and gas/water. See Mitchell and Deane, 60.

4 Taken from Routh, 8. Class 1 are professionals, Class 2 employers and managers, Class 3 clerical workers, Class 4 foremen and supervisors, Classes 5–7 manual workers.

5 *Social Trends* (1984), 129.

6 *Ibid.*, 129.

7 On this subject see above, pp. 72–80 and Milward, *passim*.

8 See, for example, Pollard, 'Trade Unions', *passim*; Allen, *passim*; Saville, *passim*.

9 Additionally, the social origins of 23 per cent were unknown. I should note that I disagree considerably with these findings, and have found much more evidence of upward social mobility in my own research into the social origins of these same men. See Rubinstein, 'Education' and also Perkin, 151–67, esp. 164–7.

10 It should be noted, however, that 51 per cent of these chairmen born in 1840–59, 43 per cent born in 1860–79, and 34 per cent born in 1880–99 attended Eton or Harrow.

11 Some of the firms and names mentioned in this extract may possibly

be unfamiliar to readers. Hambro's, Lazards, Rothschilds, and Morgan Grenfell are old and world famous merchant banks in the City of London; Shaw, Saville and Albion, the Aberdeen and Commonwealth Line and Furness Withy are large shipping companies. Dalgety's is a firm of merchants. R.A. Butler was Tory Home Secretary at the time. A number of firms mentioned here have since merged and changed their name, e.g. Consolidated Zinc is now Rio Tinto Zinc, etc.

IV. *Economic equality: Britain and the world – some comparisons*

1 Piggott, *passim*. See also Rubinstein, 'Distribution', *passim* and Harrison, *passim*.

Bibliography

Aaronovitch, S., *Monopoly: A Study of British Monopoly Capitalism*, London, 1955

Abel-Smith, Brian, and Townsend, P., *The Poor and the Poorest*, London, 1965

Abrahamson, Mark, Mizruchi, Ephraim H. and Hornburg, Carlton A., *Stratification and Mobility*, New York, 1976

Aldcroft, Derek H., *The British Economy Between the Wars*, Oxford, 1983

Allen, V.L., 'Trade Unions in Contemporary Capitalism', in Miliband, Ralph and Saville, John, eds., *Socialist Register 1964*, London, 1965

Althusser, Louis, *For Marx*, London, 1977

Atkinson, A.B., *The Economics of Inequality*, Oxford, 1975

—, ed., *Wealth, Income, and Inequality*, Harmondsworth, 1973

—, ed., *Wealth, Income, and Inequality*, Oxford, 1980

— and Harrison, A.J., *The Distribution of Personal Wealth in Britain*, Cambridge, 1978

Bacon, Robert W. and Eltis, W.A., *Britain's Economic Problem: Too Few Producers*, London, 1978

Banks, J.A., *Prosperity and Parenthood*, London, 1954

—, *Victorian Values: Secularism and the Size of Families*, London, 1981

Bateman, John, *The Great Landowners of Great Britain and Ireland* (1884; reprinted Leicester University Press, 1975)

Bendix, Reinhard and Lipset, Seymour Martin, *Social Mobility in Industrial Society*, Berkeley, 1959

Bowley, Arthur and Hogg, Margaret, *Has Poverty Diminished?*, London, 1924

Burnett, John, *Plenty and Want: A Social History of Diet in England from 1815 to the Present Day*, Harmondsworth, 1966

Butler, David and Sloman, Anne, *British Political Facts 1900–1975*, London, 1975

Camp, Anthony J., *Wills and Their Whereabouts*, London, 1974

Cappelli, Peter, *What People Earn: The Book of Wages and Salaries*, London, 1981

Coleman, D.C., 'Gentlemen and Players', *Economic History Review*, 2nd ser., 26, 1973

Cook, Chris and Keith, Brendan, *British Historical Facts 1830–1900*, London, 1975

Cowling, Maurice, *The Impact of Labour, 1920–24*, Cambridge, 1971

Crossick, Geoffrey, ed., *The Lower Middle Class in Britain, 1870–1914*, London, 1977

Dahrendorf, Ralf, *Class and Class Conflict in Industrial Society*, London, 1959

Daniels, G.W. and Campion, H., *The Distribution of National Capital*, Manchester 1936

Davis, Kingsley and Moore, W.E., 'Some Principles of Stratification', *American Sociological Review* 10, 1945

Deane, Phyllis, *The First Industrial Revolution*, Cambridge, 1965

— and Cole, W.A., *British Economic Growth, 1688–1959*, Cambridge, 1969

Duman, Daniel, *The Judicial Bench in England 1727–1875: The Reshaping of a Professional Elite* (Royal Historical Society, London, 1982)

Dunn, A.L. and Hoffman, P.D.R.B., 'The Distribution of Personal Wealth', *Economic Trends*, November 1978

Field, Frank, ed., *The Wealth Report*, London, 1979

Flinn, M.W., *The Origins of the Industrial Revolution*, New York, 1966

Galbraith, G.V., *The New Industrial State*, London, 1967

Gathorne-Hardy, Jonathan, *The Old School Tie: The Phenomenon of the English Public School*, New York, 1977

Gatrell, V.A.C., 'Labour, Power, and the Size of Firms in Lancashire Cotton in the Second Quarter of the Nineteenth Century', *Economic History Review*, 2nd ser., 30, 1977

Gerth, H.H. and Wright Mills, C., *From Max Weber: Essays in Sociology*, London, 1948

Glass, D.V., ed., *Social Mobility in Britain*, London, 1954

Glynn, Sean, and Oxborrow, John, *Interwar Britain: A Social and Economic History*, London, 1976

Goldthorpe, J.H., *Social Mobility and Class Structure in Modern Britain*, Oxford, 1980

Gosden, P.H.J.H., *Self-Help: Voluntary Associations in the Nineteenth Century*, London, 1973

Griffiths, David, Review of Stephen Merrett and Fred Gray, *Owner Occupation in Britain*, *New Socialist* No. 13, September/October 1983

Haig, Alan, *The Victorian Clergy*, Beckenham, 1984

Harbury, C.D., 'Inheritance and the Distribution of Personal Wealth in Britain', *Economic Journal* 72, 1962

— and Hitchens, D.M.W.N., *Inheritance and Wealth Inequality in Britain*, London, 1979

— and MacMahon, P.C., 'Intergenerational Wealth Transmission and the Characteristics of Top Wealth Leavers in Britain', in Stanworth, Philip and Giddens, Anthony, *Elites and Power in British Society*, Cambridge, 1974

Harrison, A., 'The Distribution of Wealth in Ten Countries', Royal Commission on the Distribution of Income and Wealth, 'Background Paper to Report No. 7', 1979

Hay, Douglas, *et al.*, *Albion's Fatal Tree: Crime and Society in Eighteenth Century England*, Harmondsworth, 1977

Heath, Anthony, *Social Mobility*, London, 1981

Holmes, G.S., 'Gregory King and the Social Structure of Pre-industrial England', *Transactions of the Royal Statistical Society*, 5th ser., 27, 1976

Honey, J.R.DeS., *Tom Brown's Universe: The Development of the Victorian Public School*, London, 1977

Hunt, E.H., *Regional Wage Variations In Britain, 1850–1914*, Oxford, 1973

Jones, Aubrey, ed., *Economics and Equality*, Oxford, 1976

Joyce, Patrick, *Work, Society, and Politics: The Culture of the Factory In Later Victorian England*, London, 1980

Kuczynski, Jurgen, *A Short History of Labour Conditions Under Industrial*

Capitalism in Great Britain and the Empire, 1750–1944, 2 volumes, London, 1946

Kuznets, Simon, 'Economic Growth and Income Inequality', *American Economic Review* 45, 1955

Langley, Kathleen M., 'The Distribution of Capital in Private Hands in 1936–8 and 1946–7', *Bulletin of the Institute of Statistics,* Oxford, 1950

Lewis, Roy and Maude, Angus, *The English Middle Classes,* Harmondsworth, 1950

Lindert, Peter H., *Lucrens Angliae: The Distribution of English Private Wealth Since 1760* (forthcoming)

— and Williamson, Jeffrey G., 'Revising England's Social Tables, 1688–1867', Working Paper Series No. 176, Department of Economics, University of California, Davis, California, September 1981

—, 'Reinterpreting Britain's Social Tables, 1688–1913', *Explorations in Economic History* 20 (1983)

Lipton, Tom and Wilson, C. Shirley, 'The Social Background and Connections of "Top Decision Makers"', *The Manchester School* 27, 1959

MacFarlane, Alan, *The Origins of English Individualism: The Family, Property and Social Transition,* Oxford, 1978

Mathias, Peter, 'The Social Structure in the Eighteenth Century: A Calculation by Joseph Massie', *Economic History Review,* 2nd ser., 10, 1957

Middlemas, Keith, *Politics in Industrial Society: The Experience of the British System Since 1911,* London, 1979

Miliband, Ralph, *The State in Capitalist Society,* London, 1973

Milward, Alan S., *The Economic Effects of the Two World Wars On Britain,* London, 1970

Mitchell, B.R. and Deane, Phyllis, *Abstract of British Historical Statistics,* Cambridge, 1971

Musgrove, Frank, 'Middle-Class Education and Employment in the Nineteenth Century', *Economic History Review,* 2nd ser., 12 (1959–60)

Offer, Avner, *Property and Politics 1870–1914: Landownership, Law, Ideology, and Urban Development,* Cambridge, 1983

Parkin, Frank, *Marxism and Class Theory,* London, 1979

Payne, P.L., 'The Emergence of the Large-Scale Company in Great Britain 1870–1914', *Economic History Review*, 2nd ser., 20, 1967

Perkin, Harold, 'Middle-Class Education and Employment in the Nineteenth Century: A Critical Note', *Economic History Review*, 2nd ser., 20, 1961–2

—, *The Origins of Modern English Society*, London, 1969

Petersen, M. Jeanne, *The Medical Profession in Mid-Victorian London*, Berkeley, 1978

Piggott, John, 'The Distribution of Wealth in Australia – A Survey' *Economic Record*, Survey Series (forthcoming)

Polanyi, George and Wood, John B., *How Much Inequality?*, Institute of Economic Affairs, London, Research Monograph no. 31, 1974

Pollard, Sidney, 'Trade Unions and the Labour Market, 1870–1914', *Yorkshire Bulletin of Economic and Social Research*, 1965

—, *The Wasting of the British Economy*, New York, 1982

Poulantzas, Nicholas, *Classes in Contemporary Capitalism*, London, 1975

Reader, William J., *Professional Men: The Rise of the Professional Classes in Nineteenth Century England*, London, 1966

Report of the Royal Commission on the Distribution of Income and Wealth, H.M.S.O., London, 1976–9

Routh, Guy, *Occupation and Pay in Great Britain, 1906–79*, London, 1980

Rubinstein, W.D. 'The Distribution of Personal Wealth in Victoria, 1860–1974', *Australian Economic History Review* 19, 1979

—, 'Education and the Social Origins of British Elites, 1880–1970', *Past and Present* (forthcoming, 1986)

—, 'The End of "Old Corruption" in Britain, 1760–1850', *Past and Present*, 101, 1983

—, *Men of Property: The Very Wealthy In Britain Since the Industrial Revolution*, London, 1981

—, 'Wealth Elites, and the Class Structure of Modern Britain', *Past and Present*, 77, 1977

Sampson, Anthony J., *The Changing Anatomy of Britain*, London, 1984

Saville, John, 'Labour and Income Distribution' in Ralph Miliband and John Saville, eds., *Socialist Register 1975*, London, 1975

Scott, John, *The Upper Classes: Property and Privilege in Britain*, London, 1982

— and Hughes, Michael, *The Anatomy of Scottish Capital*, London, 1980

Seers, D.G., *The Levelling of Income Since 1938*, Institute of Statistics, Oxford, 1951

Selsam, Howard, Goldway, David and Martel, Harry, *Dynamics of Social Change: A Reader in Marxist Social Science*, New York, 1970

Social Trends No. 13 H.M.S.O., London, 1983

Social Trends No. 14 H.M.S.O., London, 1984

Soltow, Lee, 'Long-Run Changes in British Income Inequality', *Economic History Review*, 2nd. ser., 21 (1968, reprinted in Atkinson, A.B. ed. (*q.v.*)

Stamp, Josiah, 'British Income and Property', London, 1916

Stanworth, Philip and Giddens Anthony, eds., *Elites and Power in British Society*, Cambridge, 1974

Stark, Thomas, *The Distribution of Personal Income in the United Kingdom 1949–1963* (1972) *Statistical Abstract of the United States, 1982–83*, Washington, DC, 1982

Stevenson, John, *British Society, 1914–45*, Harmondsworth, 1984

Stevenson, T.H.C., 'The Fertility of Various Social Classes in England and Wales from the Middle of the Nineteenth Century to 1911', *Journal of the Royal Statistical Society* 83, 1920

Swenarton, Mark C. and Taylor, Sandra A., 'The Scale and Nature of the Growth of Owner-Occupation in Britain *c.* 1890–1939' (unpublished)

Thomas, Ceri, 'Family and Kinship in Eaton Square' in Frank Field, ed., *The Wealth Report*, London, 1979

Thompson, F.M.L., *English Landed Society In the Nineteenth Century*, London, 1963

Titmuss, Richard M., *Income Distribution and Social Change*, London, 1962

Urry, John and Wakeford, John, eds., *Power in Britain: Sociological Readings*, London, 1973

Webb, Beatrice, *My Apprenticeship*, 2 vols., London, 1938

Wedderburn, Dorothy, ed., *Poverty, Inequality, and Class Structure*, Cambridge, 1974

Wedgwood, Josiah, *The Economics of Inheritance*, London, 1929

Westergaard, John, 'Class of '84', *New Socialist* No. 15, January/February 1984

— and Resler, H., *Class in a Capitalist Society*, Harmondsworth, 1976

Whitley, Richard, 'The City and Industry: the Directors of Large Companies, their Characteristics and Connections', in Stanworth and Giddens

Wiener, Martin, *English Culture and the Decline of the Industrial Spirit, 1850–1980*, Cambridge, 1982

Wood, John B., *How Much Inequality?*, Institute of Economic Affairs Research Monograph No. 31, 1974

Index

agriculture, employment in, 116–7
Aldcroft, Derek, 74, 77–8
aristocracy, British, privileges, 21–2, 32–3
European, 22
Atkinson, A.B., 95
Australia, comparisons with Britain, 150–1
home ownership in, 102, 151
wealth distribution in, 150–1

Bank of England, 137–8
Bank Rate Tribunal (1957), 137
barristers, role of, 34–5
Baxter, Dudley, 59, 64
Bill of Rights, 25, 32
Booth, Charles, 74, 133
Bowley, Arthur, 59, 74–5, 77
building societies, 125–6

capitalism, effects on income distribution, 110–12
Civil Service, 16, 30
clergymen, Anglican, 16, 35
Colquhoun, Patrick, 59, 65, 67
Conservative Party, 12, 28, 43, 76, 103–11, 135
consumer durables, ownership of, 84–5, 100

Depression of 1930s, 76–8, 102, 133
Diamond Commission, 78–80

economic equality, 41–3
economic growth, effects on income distribution, 108–10
failure in Britain, 99–100
education, higher, in modern Britain, 122
equality (*see also* inequality)
economic, in Britain, 41–3
legal, in Britain, 20–45
political, in Britain, 25–31
'psychological', 26–7
social, in Britain, 31–41
electorate, expansion of, 26–8
Ellerman, Sir John, 136, 140, 144
elitism, theory of inequality, 17–18
'Establishment', nature of, 134–8

family size, decline of, 113–16
First World War, 16, 39, 41, 65, 72–8, 88, 107, 128–9
friendly societies, 92
functionalism, theory of inequality, 18–19

'gentlemen', code of, 33–4
Gini coefficient, defined, 66

Harrison, A.J., 95
House of Lords, 21–2, 26, 30–1, 41
home ownership, by non-whites, 105
Labour view of, 103–4

[165]